SEEKING FREEDOM

BY

YEMA LUCILDA HUNTER

Published by SONDIATA GLOBAL MEDIA Ltd
(Songlome)

Copyright © Yema Lucilda Hunter 2016-
Second Edition

First published as Road to Freedom by African
Universities Press, Ibadan, Nigeria in 1982.

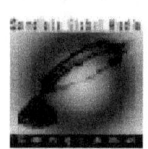

Cover design by Mark Hunter Colleone.com .. JAH
RastaFAR I.... C LA C I adapted by Khadi Mansaray
http://www.sondiataglobalmedia.com

CONTENTS

Introduction

Before I married Mr. Rupert Androver, he told me that his most pressing ambition was to attempt to classify the flowers of West Africa. It was therefore no surprise to me when, early in 1820, he announced that he intended to visit our colony, Freetown, on that part of the West African coast known as Sierra Leone.

Since we had been married only a year at the time and had as yet had produced no off-spring, I expressed a desire to accompany him. At first Mr. Androver was adamant in his refusal, saying he would not expose his precious wife to the hazards of a place known as 'the white man's grave'. However, I was determined not to be excluded from such an adventure and whittled down his resistance in all the ways at the disposal of a resourceful woman. In the end he relented, albeit reluctantly, and we sailed out there that October.

We stayed in Freetown for two years, but I experienced no moments of regret. I did suffer from a virulent fever more than once and each time emerged from the experience limp of body and sallow of skin, but I was firm in my decision not to return to England without Mr. Androver. I caused him great anxiety and vexation, no doubt, but he had to admit that the tints of colour I added to his plain sketches greatly improved their interest and value.

In spite of the climate, which is indeed

uncomfortable, being hot and humid in the extreme, and the ants, flies and mosquitoes which are a constant torment, Freetown has a certain indefinable charm. It is a small, quaint, coastal town set against a startling backdrop of steep, thickly wooded hills. In the centre of the town another hill rises, and on its slopes stands, appropriately, the fortress home of the Governor of the colony.

Gorgeously coloured flowers and lush vegetation constantly delight the eye and every part of the town affords a pleasing prospect of the Atlantic Ocean. There are a few stone houses, but most of the dwellings are of the wooden frame type. Some are raised off the ground on stone cellars to keep out the damp and the many crawling creatures that hide in the nooks and crannies of dwelling houses. The well-to-do use slate or shingle for their roofs, while the poor use either grass or beautifully plaited and trimmed leaves of the palm tree.

Without doubt, though, the most fascinating aspect of the place is it population. There are some Europeans, but so few that I must have encountered most of them. Everyone else is either a native African or of African descent. The natives, called Timmanees or Temnes, may be recognised by their exotic apparel, or, in the case of the women, scanty apparel. They do not live in Freetown itself, but in nearby hamlets, arriving each day to trade in foodstuffs, to work as labourers and servants, or in the case of children, to attend school. The rest of the population is made up of settlers of one kind or another, all living clannishly in their own sections of the town, though there is much intermingling during the day. Fulas, slender and thin - featured and not as dark-skinned as the Timmanees, live somewhere to the east, I believe. The women have wonderfully tender faces and their infants are adorable cherubs. Most of the Fula men I saw were habitually attired in long robes of white, or blue, similar to nightshirts, and seemed almost always to be in the company of emaciated cows.

In another section of the town live the Krus, men of a rough, tough appearance. They are, for the most part, labourers, or seamen. I understand that they fiercely resisted all attempts to sell them into slavery, preferring to die when captured. Their womenfolk are also remarkably muscular and fond of coating their faces with a chalky substance which I believe to be a kind of beauty mask. Settlers from Jamaica, known as Maroons and settlers from Nova Scotia live in the central parts of the town. Others, known as Recaptives, or Liberated Africans, were rescued from slavers by British warships patrolling along the west coast. They were resettled in Freetown and have their dwellings around the Maroon and Nova Scotian settlements, and also in hamlets to the east, to the west, and in the hills. During my sojourn in Freetown, their arrival in large numbers was almost a daily occurrence. It is easy to recognise newly arrived Recaptives on account of their wretched and ragged appearance, but those who have overcome the distress of being kidnapped and the bewilderment of finding themselves far from home, move around with remarkable vigour and purpose. In ten years they may present a different picture to the visitor.

I was informed that the Maroons are the most unfriendly and belligerent of the settlers, while the Nova Scotians have the most languidly aristocratic bearing. Nova Scotian women adore brightly coloured bonnets and the men often sport beaver hats.

Despite the heat, gloves are de rigueur for stepping out into the street on a Sunday afternoon. But for their sable complexions, they would not be out of place in the streets of one of our provincial towns.

I became friendly with one of them, a Mrs. Deannie Porter, whom I met by chance one afternoon some weeks after our arrival. Freetown has a small subscription library and I had gone to browse among the shelves while awaiting Mr. Androver's return from an excursion up the slopes of one of the nearby hills. Mrs. Porter came in to return a book, and being of a very inquisitive disposition, and also not a little startled that she should be in the library at all, I could not help but peep to see what book she had come to return. It was Daniel Defoe's Moll Flanders. To say I was surprised would be to put it mildly, for I had been of the opinion that the settlers possessed at best but the rudiments of education. I could not resist asking her how she had enjoyed the novel, fully expecting her to say that she had found it somewhat hard going. She replied politely, but with cool reserve that she had enjoyed it well enough, though she found Robinson Crusoe a more interesting book and wondered if I agreed with her.

'You have read that also?' I asked, thoroughly intrigued by that time.

'Indeed I have, Madam.' Her eyes twinkled. 'I have been through many a book in my time.'

'Are you perhaps a school teacher?' I asked.

She chuckled, 'I suppose you are surprised to meet anAfrican who can read.'

'No, no,' I hastened to say, 'but...but I did not expect to find a busy housewife as I know you must be, having the time to read. Back home in England, we can leave the running of our households to well-trained servants, but here I have to supervise my servants at every turn...You must be a remarkable woman.'

This time she laughed louder, and her shell of reserve cracked.

'Not in the least remarkable. It is simply that I have a passion for stories. Sometimes I vex my husband so much with my reading that he says I'm just a busy - body at heart.'

That was how our acquaintance began, and before long we had become friends. It was on another occasion that Mrs. Porter told me how she had come over to Africa from Nova Scotia in 1792. She learned to read long before she arrived in Freetown, but it was after a town library was started under one of the early governors that she developed a taste for novels.

Several conversations later, I said to her, 'You ought to write your life story, you know - at least something about the years when you first came here. I find it absolutely fascinating to listen to you.'

'Oh, no, that would be far too difficult for me!' she replied at once, astonished at the suggestion. However, her expression assumed a certain thoughtfulness which made me suspect that she had begun to entertain the notion.

From time to time when we met after that, I would say, in a jesting fashion, 'And how is the story progressing?' Mrs. Porter never did more than laugh in a way that revealed nothing; and then she would change the subject.

Came the day Mr. Androver and I were about to leave Freetown for good. Mrs. Porter arrived at the wharf with her younger children to bid me goodbye. At the very last moment, just before I boarded the boat that would row us out to our ship, she handed me a flat rectangular package, saying,

'I hope this will help while away the time on board.'

From its shape and size, I guessed at once what the package contained.

'Mrs. Porter! You have done it!' I cried.

'Yes,' she said, somewhat shyly, 'it was a change from reading, and it did me a power of good; but I must beg you to share it only with your friends. It is not my wish to cause embarrassment to any person still living.'

I gave her my assurances and we said goodbye.

I later received permission from Mrs. Porter for the manuscript to be published if future generations of my family so desired, but only after sixty years had elapsed. By that time all who have played an active part in its pages should either have crossed over to the next world, or have ceased to concern themselves with what takes place in this one.

Petrina Androver
1823

PART ONE

Chapter 1
The coming of the stranger

Sunday, the fifteenth day of May, in the year of our Lord seventeen hundred and ninety-one, began like any other Sunday in our household, but subsequent events were to prove it a day of extraordinary significance. Naturally, none of us had any inkling of its importance at six o'clock that morning.

I was forced to surface from the depths of sleep by my mother calling out,

'Rise an' shine', rise an' shine you lazy tin'. You forgettin' today de Lord's Day? ... Come on now, get up. You know when Bro come in from de washhouse he goin' be ready for prayers.'

She came over and shook me till I opened my eyes, which I did only with reluctance; I had been snug and warm in the cocoon of my blanket. I lay there groaning and rubbing my eyes with my fists; she grasped my shoulders and forced me to sit up before going over to my brother Daniel's pallet to give him the same treatment. Daniel rose almost at once and stumbled out into the yard to ease himself. My mother had already made up the fire, but its warmth had not yet reached my corner of the room. The frosty air on my shoulders woke me fully, but instead of rising, I proceeded to yawn hugely and loudly, stretching my arms like a lazy kitten. At the other end of the room my mother was busy mixing oats in the smoke-blackened pot, but she realised what I was doing and said, without much raising her voice,

'You, Deannie, if you don' get out dat bed dis very minute I goin' warm you' behine for you; ... don' care if you tirteen today.'

It was my birthday! I sprang out of bed and ran across the room to throw my arms around my mother from behind. I laid my cheek against her broad soft back and hugged her with all my strength.

'Mammy,' I said, 'from today, I never goin' make you holler on me no more. I goin' show you dat I done grown up now.'

She turned and hugged me back, giving her special chuckle which seemed to come from deep inside her throat and made her shoulders shake just once.

'Dat so,' she said. 'Member what de Master say, eh? "By dey fruit ye shall know dem!"'

'Oh, Mammy! Jus' you wait an' see!'

To start proving myself, I whirled about our cabin, setting it to rights; shook my pallet, and shoved it against the wall, shook up Daniel's, put it on top of mine, then spread our worn blankets over them with exaggerated care. My mother was very particular that there should be no wrinkles in the blankets.

In those far away days, we lived in Birchtown on the Atlantic coast of Nova Scotia, in a community of about two thousand Negroes, freed slaves for the most part. There were just the four of us in our family. At the head, was my father. His name was Jabez Dixon, but we always called him 'Bro', short for, Brother Dixon; after him, my lovely mother. Her name was Rebecca, but not even Bro called her that. She was Mammy to us all. My only brother, Daniel, already mentioned, was sixteen that year. He was, and is, a calm sort of person who seldom speaks unless he is first addressed.

Bro never remembered our birthdays, Daniel's or mine, and that morning was no different. As happened each year, this scene took place: morning prayers began as usual; Daniel read some verses from the Bible (sometimes I performed this duty as neither of our parents was lettered), then we went down on our knees and Bro led us in prayer. The instant we said 'Amen', I waited with amusement for Mammy's voice; sure enough, she spoke up before Bro could begin the Lord's Prayer.

'An' now Lord, look down on dis you chile, Deannie, who you been give we, today make tirteen year. We tankin' you for her life an' we pray let you spare her one more year to serve you in dis worl'.'

When we rose from our knees, Bro put an arm around my shoulders and, with a somewhat shamefaced expression, gave me a warm squeeze. As he never failed to do, he said, 'One year done pass already; don' time run on.'

As always, we laughed together, then hastened to eat our porridge. Like most of the people in Birchtown, the Dixon family was too poor for any further notice to be taken of birthdays.

It must have been about eight o'clock in the morning when we set out down the river road for the meeting - house. It was late spring, but at that time of the morning, the air was still keen enough for me to have to catch my breath when first I stepped outside. It is strange that I have no recollection of how I was dressed that day, yet can still picture Mammy with her heavy man's coat over a purple wool gown, her moth-eaten beaver hat worn over a crisp white kerchief, and her usually animated face quietly composed beneath. Thus had she prepared herself for the hours of spiritual refreshment that lay ahead. Bro also had on a beaver hat, but Daniel's head was covered by a knitted cap such as was once popular with sailors. They both wore heavy coats over their breeches. Daniel had acquired his as a gift from Bro's employer some three years previously, and when he first began to wear it, his hands had been lost in the sleeves. My first sight of him thus attired provoked such a fit of giggling that he had boxed my ears in vexation and Mammy told me that I well deserved the rebuke. By the time this story begins, his hands were fully visible.

In contrast to my mother, who was brown in complexion, short and plump, Bro was a tall, black, bony man, His back was a little stooped from many years of bending over a carpenter's table. This added to the air he possessed of a man of weighty responsibilities. When we walked to the meeting - house on a Sunday morning, he held his old leather-bound Bible clasped to his chest and slowed his usually brisk pace of walking to a more dignified tread.

There was never any conversation on the journeys to the meeting-house; Bro had decreed that talking did not prepare us for entering the presence of the Lord. I did not mind the enforced silence for I always found much to interest my eyes as we walked along. I am also certain that Daniel was well content not to have to take part in a conversation. Mammy, on the other hand, must have suffered a little since she was the one member of our family given to much speech. Yet no one would have guessed that the enforced silence was a strain by looking at her — her countenance on those journeys remained as serene as the ocean on a windless day.

The meeting - house was not far from where we lived, and before long we began to see the curling shingles of its roof and its log-hewn walls. It was a roughly constructed building with wooden pews on either side of a narrow aisle from the door to within four or five feet of the altar which was a beautifully carved wooden table Bro had made. Behind the altar a large wooden cross had been nailed to the wall, and to the left of it stood a lectern, carved in the same design. It was from this vantage point that Brother Isaacs, our church leader, read aloud from the Bible and delivered stern sermons.

A wide but fairly shallow river flowed along one side of the meeting-house. Here it was that people were immersed for baptism, for ours was a small Baptist congregation. The main Baptist Church was in Shelburne Town, a community mostly of whitefolk, one or two miles away. Its leader, Pastor David George, led a flourishing congregation composed almost entirely of Negroes, but including a few white members of that community. It was the same Pastor George who had started the Baptist Church in Birchtown but he had, in some way never made clear to me, fallen foul of some of the influential members of our community and forced to make a hasty departure. He left behind a faithful flock of converts who, with their families, totalled about fifty persons. We continued to meet in the little chapel he built.

Our Sunday services never lasted less than three hours, but with our lively manner of worship, the time passed like a few minutes. We always made a joyful noise unto the Lord - swaying and clapping as well as singing at the tops of our voices, and it was a common occurrence for several individuals to be seized by the Holy Spirit in the middle of a prayer or a hymn. They would suddenly shout out in strange tongues, or shake from head to foot. Some members of the congregation even fell to the ground, thrashing about in ecstasy. I had seen it happen three times to Mammy and once to Bro, but at that time, I had never yet experienced this mystical visitation. The Holy Spirit did not seem to come to people of less than mature years.

I recollect one member of our congregation who, at every service, never failed to be moved by the Spirit in one way, or another. Her name was Sister Clarissa King, and her image remains fixed in my mind. She was shorter than Mammy, as dark as molasses and enormously stout; all in all, she reminded me of a large black chest. I was able to observe her without hindrance because she sat with her husband one pew in front of us and across the aisle. The holy visitations left her exhausted and, expecting every gasping breath to be her last, I would watch in fearful fascination as her pillow of a bosom rose and fell like a dinghy on a rough sea. While she panted, her immense, sagging arms lay collapsed at her sides, palms facing upwards, which gave her the proper air of abandonment to the will of the Lord.

Sister King's husband was a small, light-skinned man, who hardly opened his little mouth when he sang, and barely touched his fingertips together when he clapped. Never to my knowledge, had he experienced the Holy Spirit, but whenever his wife was thus transported, I would observe his lips quietly mouthing the words, 'Hallelujah! Hallelujah!' And when, finally, she sank into her seat gasping and spent, it was always moving, though somewhat comical, to see the tenderness with which he bent down to pat her dripping face and fan her with his scarlet handkerchief.

That Sunday, the service proceeded in its usual manner until the final prayer when, raising his voice with even greater fervour than was his wont, Brother Isaacs said,

'An' now, Lord, we pray you goin' look down on we broda, Thomas Peters, who visitin' Birchtown today, an' who in a little while goin' face danger on de wide open sea.'

'Who Thomas Peters?' I whispered to Daniel; he shrugged his shoulders. The chapel hummed like a hundred bumblebees as the same question went from person to person. It seemed that most of the congregation had no idea that there was a stranger in Birchtown, let alone one called Thomas Peters. The disturbance forced Brother Isaacs to pause in his prayer for a moment, then finish in a voice like thunder.

'De Lord of Host is wit' us; de God of Jaycob is our refuge!'

After the Benediction, the meeting house hummed again. Brother Isaacs raised his hand and demanded silence, then announced that all members of the congregation were to proceed at once to the Methodist Chapel; that Brother Thomas Peters was visiting from Annapolis Royal and wished to address residents of the area.

The Methodist Chapel was on the Shelburne side of Birchtown, a short walk from our own meeting - house. It was a large, low, frame building capable of holding several hundred people. Even so, by the time we arrived, it overflowed with humanity. Only those of us with smaller frames were able to squeeze into the spaces remaining in the pews; everyone else, Bro and Mammy included, was obliged to stand at the back or along the side aisles. Up in front I could see the grizzled head of Pastor Moses Wilkinson, the Methodist leader; Bro and Mammy always referred to him as 'Daddy Moses'. Blind and lame in his left leg, he was nonetheless an awesome figure to me in his black clothes. Standing next to him was another man, whom he introduced as Thomas Peters. The stranger was in no way as impressive a figure as Daddy Moses, being rather short, and clad in a suit remarkable for its shabbiness even in our poverty-stricken community. I felt somewhat disappointed at first, but when Thomas Peters spoke, the tide of his eloquence swept my previous impression aside.

'Brodas and sistas of Birchtown,' he began in a strong, slow voice, his expression, sombre. 'I goin' tell you all a story - a story 'bout a slave man livin' down in Car'lina ... One day, dis slave been drive a wagon to town to buy supply for he master. He finish to buy de supply an' jus' gettin' ready to climb in de wagon to go home when a voice call out to him, 'Boy! Hey, boy!' De slave man turn aroun' an' he see dis white man strollin' up to de wagon. When he reaches it, he start to talk real quiet. He ask dat slave man if he lookin ' to be free. I kin tell you all, brodas and sistas, at firs' de slave man ready to jump on de wagon as quick as a rabbit an' put dust between him an' dat white man. You all know how in dem days dem plantation owner always findin' to know which slave goin' make trouble so dey kin deal wit' him good an' proper ... But again, dat white man been look differen' somehow, so, behine he heart, de slave man stop an' listen to what de white man got to say.'

Thomas Peters told us how the white man had told the slave that if he went in the night to a nearby wood he would be told how he could gain his freedom forever. Late that night, when all the plantation was safely asleep, the slave crept out to the appointed meeting place; the white man was already waiting, and they were soon joined by four other slaves. The white man told them that he was from a country called England whose king owned America, but that some of these Americans had rebelled and declared that they wanted to rule themselves. The king was determined to crush the rebellion but needed help, so the white man had been sent to promise freedom to slaves who were willing to fight on their side against the rebellious Americans. If they joined the British soldiers, they would be given their freedom at the end of the war and, in addition, receive twenty acres of good land for farming, with all profits going to their own pockets instead of to slave masters. The promise of freedom and a livelihood had been enough to persuade the young men; they decided to make good their escape without delay.

'Brodas an' sistas, dat slave man been fight wit' de Redcoat soldiers,' Thomas Peters went

on. 'Dey los' de war an' de English king los' America, but never mine; de slave man done keep he
promise. He don' fight for de king an' now he
lookin' to English people to keep dey word...
Know what happen? "Course you free now!" dey
tell him. "Here a paper to prove it ... Go on up to
Canada - to Nova Scotia; plenty fine lan' dere." An
so de slave man who now suppose to be free
been come to Nova Scotia ...Brodas an' sistas,
every tin' I done tell you happen seven year ago...
Seven year done pass from de time dat slave man
come to dis place. Till today he waitin' for he
lan'.

Thomas Peters gazed at us for several seconds without speaking. It was in silence almost
deep enough to hear grass growing outside that
we waited for him to continue.

'You all done know by now dat de slave man
I been talkin' 'bout be nobody but me; but,' he
went on, pointing to different parts of the room,
'my story de same as you story, an' you story, an'
you story, 'ceptin' maybe some of you come from
someplace else in America .. Seven long year we
done wait for we twenty acre an' only few of we
been lucky up to now. What dey tell we? Oh, dey
keep on sayin', "Be patient! Dem tin' take time."
Seven year? ... Let I ask you all now. We better
off now dan when we been slave? Anyone of you
been suffer so in Virginia or Car'lina, or wherever
you done come from? ... Dat time we all been
slave, yes, an' now we free; but what we free to
do, eh? I goin' tell you; we free to break we back
for notin'. We free to starve! Dat what we free to

do. We free to die! ... Some of we who done tired wit' dis shilly-shally bizness been come together in 'Napolis to talk 'bout it and make plan to force de gov'ment to act. Dey done pick me to go to Englan' an 'meet wit' dem people who know how to forget dey promise. I goin' tell dem what happenin' here; maybe dey don' know ... My brodas an' sisters, I askin' you all to pray for me! Pray let me reach Englan'— de water wide an' rough ... Pray let dem listen to me, an' pray let dem do sometin' for we now ...We done tired!'

Here and there, as Thomas Peters mentioned the hardships our people had experienced in Nova Scotia, loud sighs and groans of agreement, sympathy and remembered pain punctuated his sentences. As he sat down and mopped his brow, the whole congregation shouted, 'Amen! In that charged atmosphere, Daddy Moses spoke again, his voice shaking with emotion.

'I knows you all done give you offerin' to de Lord already, but I beg you, give again for a good cause. Let we give we broad sometin' to hol'. He goin' fight for all of we. I don' say you got to give now, but nex' week Broda Caleb Anderson, who you all know, goin' come knockin' on you door. He goin' visit every family one by one. Let we not forget, my children; de Good Lord help people who tryin' to help deyself.'

This talk of money broke the spell in which Thomas Peters seemed to have bound the congregation. Everyone began to speak at once, to move at once, and there was a great crush as a crowd surged towards the front of the chapel. Everyone wanted to shake hands with Thomas Peters and offer him personal good wishes. Several minutes passed before we were able to emerge from the chapel and start for home.

Chapter 2
What happened to the Dixons before

Another of Bro's firm rules was that there should be no conversation among us on our return journey from the meetinghouse; it was supposed to be a time of quiet reflection onBrother Isaac's message. On that memorable Sunday, however, by the time we were homeward bound, the morning's service
seemed to have taken place several days earlier; not even Bro could have been thinking about Brother Isaac's sermon. As was to be expected, it was Mammy who broke the rule and broached the subject uppermost in all our minds.

'Bro, what you tink 'bout what Broda Peters tell us jus' now? You tink he goin' win?'

'Mammy, don' know what to say,' Bro replied. 'Only tin' we kin do is pray like he done ask we to; ... you an' me, we know whitefolk like we know we own children. If dey do sometin' for we now it goin' be because of de Lord workin' in dey heart. Like Thomas Peters say, dey done promise befo' dat dey goin' treat we de same like dey treat all de people who done fight wit' dem, but when we reach here, is whitefolk firs' an' what dey don' want,dey give to darkies. Dem people in England whitefolk jus' like people over here. Dey not different ... I been disappoint too long, Mammy. I don' hope for notin'.'

'But you know sometin', Bro,' Mammy said, 'day befo' yesterday, I dream again. I been musin' 'bout de dream but till today I don' know de meanin'. Now I tink I knows ...'

'What you dream?' Bro asked.

'I dream I been walkin' down Shelburne Road wit' my basket, takin' clean wash to Mrs. Catchpole house. As I walkin' along, I seen one man comin' dis way like he comin' to Birchtown. In de dream, he face been mix up but I knows I never seen him befo'. When we two meet up, he ask me how to come to Birchtown an' I been show him. Den he say, "Tank you, Sister, we goin' meet again befo' long."'

'You tink de man in de dream Thomas Peters, Mammy?' I asked.

'Who else, chile? I knows dat man Thomas Peters, an' because I done dream him, I know is de Lord who done bring him here, an' if de Lord han' in it, every tin ' goin' be all right; not so, Bro?'

'You right,' Bro agreed. 'We jus' got to pray for Thomas Peters an' wait for de Lord. Notin' else to do.'

The praying began before we sat down to our meal which Mammy always prepared the previous day so as not to break the Sabbath. I was almost trembling with hunger, and the mouthwatering aroma of salted hogs' feet boiled in molasses, all but ruined my concentration as Bro brought before the Lord the case of the freed slaves in Nova Scotia. He described Thomas Peters in detail as if to make sure the Lord could recognise him in a crowd. When at last we sat down, our food was barely warm, but the Sunday meal being always the best one of the week, we still consumed it with relish. For several minutes, the only sounds in the Dixon household came from spoons scraping dishes and teeth crunching succulent bones.

I forgot about Thomas Peters for the dura- tion of the meal, but once my hunger was satis- fied, my thoughts returned to the events of the morning. I knew that Daniel and I had been born in America, but never before had Bro or Mammy encouraged questions about the past. It may have been that they did not care to remember a time when they had been slaves. It now seemed that because Thomas Peters's visit had forced them to remember that time, a barrier had been breached, making them all too willing to talk about their past and present lives.

'Like de man say, he been talkin' 'bout mos' everybody here,' Bro said in reply to a comment I cannot now remember. 'Mammy an' me, we too been come from Car'lina, but we more lucky dan many people. We master, Mr. Dixon, differen' than plenty oda slave master; he never sell slave who sharin' one cabin an' breedin' children, so when we run away we been able to go wit' we children. Don' know why, but de good Lord done bless me an' Mammy all de way. We been yard slave so we able to do other work dan jus' plantin' cotton an' rice, me wit' carpenter work, an' Mammy wit' her washin' an' ironin'... Life up here too hard for people who don' know no trade; wages whitefolk give farm han' won' fill de belly of a flea.'

'Member two years past when de famine be?' Mammy said, 'Even we done dead by now if I not washin' for Mrs.Catchpole an' she not been a good person. She give me sometin' extra to eat every week. Many, many people jus' lay down an' die in de open road when dey too weak to walk one more step.'

'But Mammy,' I asked in my innocence, 'why dem peoplenot been go back to dey master in America befo' dey die like dat? Leastways dey sure dey goin' eat.'

'To be slave again? Chile, you don' know what you sayin!' I shrank before Mammy's eyes which were flashing scorn at me. 'Don' care what Thomas Peters say. Yes, life be hard, but freedom better dan ... dan one hundred bushel of de bes' cornmeal. Like Bro say, we Master Dixon not been wicked at all. He feed we good, give we clothes, an' he not sell we like some oda master do; but when we been get de chance to run, me an' Bro, we run jus' like dat!' She snapped her fingers. 'Not so, Bro?'

'What you sayin' true, Mammy, but some people done go back,' Bro reminded her mildly.

'Dem people who go back not fit to call dey-self people!' Mammy retorted. 'Dey jus' fit be whitefolk property, like cows or horses. Don' let me hear you Daniel Dixon, or you Deannie Dixon talkin' 'bout people to go back an' be slave again, you hear me?'

'Yes, Mammy,' Daniel and I answered in a meek chorus. Yet, I had a clear recollection that Mammy herself had experienced at least one moment of bitter doubt and despair. It had happened one winter afternoon. I must have been eight or nine years old at the time. Outside our cabin it was fiercely cold and black as pitch. Inside, it was warm, but dim and depressing with the only light coming from the flickering fire and four tallow lamps. Mammy was busy with her ironing as usual while I was huddled near one of the lamps, straining my eyes over a piece of darning. Daniel was bent over one of the other lamps, reading aloud and haltingly from the Bible. He and I had learned to read at Sunday school and ever since, Bro made one of us read to him every single evening; this, in addition to our reading at morning prayers. We almost always read from the Old Testament because of its wonderful stories; in this way the family enjoyed a kind of holy entertainment.

Perhaps the blackness of that winter afternoon had wrapped itself around Mammy's heart, for she suddenly slammed down her iron, making the rest of us jerk in our seats as if we had heard a gunshot.

'Bro, what we done gain?' she burst out in a high, strained voice. 'Tell me true; what we done gain comin' to dis place?'

Surprised and disturbed, Bro said 'Mammy!...What de matter wit' you today? We free now. Dat what we done gain;...An' we two been 'gree dat freedom more precious dan easy livin'.'

He rose from his chair as he spoke and went to put his arms on Mammy's shoulders. 'You forgettin' how long befo' dem Israelite been reach Canaan lan'? Patience, Sister!'

But Mammy had refused to be so easily comforted 'Lord forgive me, Bro, but I runnin' out of patience. You 'member dat journey? 'Member how we tremblin', ... how we been tie Sheba mout' so she not cry out loud, ... how we always hungry an' how dat day, sweet Jesus, jus' like dat, my baby done gone from me?'

Mammy's eyes were streaming with tears as she spoke. In a mixture of compassion and alarm, I also began to weep, while Daniel looked on silently.

'An' den you been gone long to fight, an' I strugglin' wit' dem other two all alone ... All de time I couragin' myself, sayin', "Slave no more, ... slave no more ... When my man come back we goin' get we own farm to work ... Freedom comin' roun' de corner!" Bro, two year done pass now,' she wailed. 'Two year! Look at me. I doin' jus' what I been doin' at Master Dixon place. An' you, too, Bro. Only tin' differen' is now we got to fine we own food an' clothes ... An' dis place so perishin' col' ...'My feet swellin' an' itchin' an' I don' have notin' better to hope for...'

Bro soothed her down in just the way he had so often soothed me down when I was younger, rubbing the palm of his hand gently round and round her back until her sobs subsided. 'Look how you upsettin' Deannie', he said. ' From de day we born, you an' me been slave. Two year notin' for we. De Lord done bring we here; I jus' knows he goin' make a way for you an' me...Wait for he time.'

My mother's outburst must have been like the lancing of a boil because she soon dried her eyes with her apron and returned to her ironing, though from time to time I heard her sniff. After a while she said in her normal voice,

'Bro, in my heart, I believe every tin' you say jus' now, but sometime I kint help myself. Dem children growin' like grass; soon we goin' be ol'.

I never again saw Mammy so distressed by our circumstances. As the years progressed she became the comforter and strong tower in our home.

As for me, I had but the haziest memory of a time when we did not live in Birchtown. I remembered that northward journey like the recollection of a dream; travelling by bushy paths throughout one night, my eyes starting out of my head at the blood - chilling cries of owls yet, having been sternly forbidden to utter any cry, I could only cling more tightly to Bro's sides and neck with my arms and legs. I remembered Mammy carrying our baby sister, Sheba, slung from her neck in a sort of hammock. I remembered a house full of people who spoke in whispers; we spent perhaps a day there - a night spent in a wagon; waking with my body stiff and sore from sleeping on the hard boards. We spent many days either in the wagon or in one of those quiet houses. Then, an evening when Mammy said to Bro in a strained and frightened voice: 'Jabe, feel dis chil'; she burnin' up wit' fever!' And by next evening, Sheba lying limp and lifeless in Mammy's arms. And Mammy's chest heaving as harsh sobs tore their way out of her. I remembered the day I heard her say, 'We safe now, Jabe? No one goin' touch we no more? Then, in a voice cracked with sorrow, 'Oh, my little Sheba, my baby!' And Bro falling to his knees and saying, 'Praise God! Praise God!' yet weeping also.

There had been several more days of travelling before we came to a large town which I heard them call Boston. Here we stayed until the war was over. Finally, when Bro returned from the battlefield, we were put on a ship, an overcrowded, ill - smelling vessel, and transported to Nova Scotia, first to Shelburne and from thence to Birchtown. All I remembered of the sea journey itself was how my belly heaved with every roll of the ship.

When we first arrived in Birchtown, we had to live in a tent for two weeks before Bro was able to complete a permanent home for us; but like most children, Daniel and I were soon accustomed to our new life, the old life all but forgotten. Our one - room log cabin was always warm enough from the ever-present fire smouldering under Mammy's flat-irons and I was happily unaware of my parents' struggle to keep our bellies filled and clothes on our backs. Oh, we saw the beggars who dragged out a wretched existence in Birchtown and Shelburne - gauntcheeked and red-eyed creatures with rusty, matted hair, clad in an astonishing assortment of stinking rags. Many of them were half-mad or crippled. They were simply dirty beggars to me - part of Birchtown's landscape, and I always wondered why Mammy insisted on giving them more food than we could easily spare when they came to our door.

Occasionally, I accompanied her to deliver the clean laundry. If we chanced upon a group of children yelling insulting rhymes and pelting sticks and stones at a beggar, Mammy's rage was a sight to behold. Clutching her heavy basket to her head with one hand, she would swoop down on those children like the Lord's avenging angel, lashing out with the other hand if any of them came within her reach. She had given Daniel and me strict warnings against taunting beggars, saying, 'Dey God's children jus' like you an' me.' On the Sunday when we first made the acquaintance of Thomas Peters, I better understood the reason for her fierce protection of them. I realised, for the first time, that for Mammy beggars might have been reminders of how much the Lord had blessed her family, but they were also examples of people who preferred freedom with hardship to bondage, no matter how carefree their bondage had been.

Chapter 3
What happened next

In Birchtown, rumours were the spice of life. Roadside encounters between neighbours and acquaintances seldom took place without, 'Hear what dey sayin' now?' forming part of the conversation. This, 'Hear what dey sayin' now' travelled in excited whispers from house to house. It became the subject of heated arguments at mealtimes, the source of many a jest, and sometimes the stuff of nightmares. The rumour current at the time of Thomas Peters's visit had noised it around the community that young Negroes were being seized in Shelburne to be sold again into slavery on West Indian plantations. It may have happened that a desperate mother used the threat to deter an errant son. Who can ever tell where a rumour begins? However, although the truth of it was never confirmed, journeys into Shelburne were now undertaken with a good deal of anxiety. Even in Birchtown, where a white person would have been as conspicuous as a flag on a barren hilltop, my mother kept a watchful eye on me. If, for any reason, she did not choose for me to accompany her to Shelburne, I was under strict instructions to remain indoors until her return.

On the following Tuesday, there was a great pile of mending to be attended to so Mammy went to Shelburne alone to deliver the clean linen. Daniel and my father were not yet returned from Mr Fowlis's carpentry shop where they were employed, my father as a carpenter and Daniel as an apprentice. I was, therefore, on my own, plying my needle with great industry when I heard a hoarse voice calling out, 'Good day, good people.'

I jumped up and peeped out of the window to see whothe visitor might be, and beheld Brother Caleb Anderson panting on the doorstep.

Poor Brother Caleb! He was old and weary, yet so great was his devotion to Pastor Wilkinson and the church that he was ever the first person to offer his services for errands; and he would have been deeply wounded to have had them refused. As a result, he was often to be seen thumping his two walking sticks as he trudged up and down the dusty, and often muddy, lanes of Birchtown, out of breath but joyfully serving the Lord.

'A fine afternoon to you, lil sister,' he said, when I opened the door to him. 'I collectin' for Broda Peters like how Pastor Wilkinson been say.'

'Come in Broda Caleb,' I said. 'Come on in an' rest youself.' I showed him to my father's chair by the fireplace. 'Mammy goin' come back jus' now an' Bro too, maybe. Let I give you some hackberry wine Mammy done make?'

'Won' say no to dat, lil sista,' Brother Caleb said as he sank into the chair. 'Goin' up an' down like dis not so easy for a ol' creature like me.'

I brought him the wine out of the stone jar where Mammy kept it and he was loud in his appreciation, asking me my name and praising my hospitality. When he had refreshed himself he leaned back in my father's chair, heaved a sigh or two and in no time at all had sunk into a deep sleep, giving out snores that began with a whistle and ended with a quiet growl. The grey tufts of hair growing out of his ears quivered with every snore, so I was giggling as I returned to my sewing. Several minutes passed before I heard Mammy calling,

'Deannie, Dea...nnie'; her voice always rose piercingly on the second shout. It was a signal for me to run outside to help her put down the wicker basket in which she carried the laundry. I told her that Brother Caleb had arrived to collect for Thomas Peters, and before I could add that he was fast asleep, she called from outside, 'How you doin' today Broda Caleb?'

As was to be expected, there was no reply.

'He sleepin', Mammy,' I informed her with another giggle. 'I been give him some of dat hackberry wine; if you hear how he snorin'.'

When we entered the house Mammy bent over Brother Caleb and said in a loud whisper, 'Broda Caleb... Broda Caleb...'

He awoke with such a start that I wondered how far his dreams had taken him in that short time. He stared at Mammy in a dazed fashion for a moment, as if he had never before set eyes on a creature of her description.

'Is Rebecca Dixon, Broda Caleb', Mammy said, speaking slowly as if to a small child. 'You in my house an' I been askin' how 'you feelin' today.'

'Oh, Sista Dixon!' he exclaimed with a shamefaced chuckle. 'Feelin' fine today; ... not ready for plantin', yet, but you lil Deannie done make me feel so easy wit' dat good wine, I done forget I suppose to be workin'.' He began to struggle out of the chair, but Mammy pressed him back.

'Sit awhile; where you runnin' to? ...I sure you tired like a mule ... 'Bout dis collection for Broda Peters ... Me and my man, we don' have no money, so we done talk dis tin' over. We done pray 'bout it an' we done make up we mine to give de only tin' we kin give to help de work of de Lord.'

As she was speaking, Mammy went behind the curtain that separated my parents' bed from the rest of the cabin. I heard her pull out the creaking drawers of the old bureau near the bed, and could hardly believe my eyes when she emerged holding her wedding ring and my father's golden studs in the palm of her hand.

If there was one thing Mammy treasured on this earth it was her wedding ring. It only graced her finger on Sundays - the one day in the week on which she washed no clothes. Once, when I remarked on this, she said, 'Deannie, girl, dis ring you see' more dan jus' a little piece of gold. I loves it more dan everytin' in dis whole worl', after you an' Danny an' you daddy, an' bein' a free woman. I not goin' put no lye soap on it. When we been slave, Bro an' me been live in one cabin but we not been wedded befo' de Lord. Is only when we done reach dis place dat we been join de Baptis' Church an' we been wed good an' proper. Is Mrs Catchpole been give me dis gold ring an' dem stud for Bro, an' I never goin' part wit' it.' I remembered how lovingly she had polished the ring against her skirt that day and then held it up to the window to catch the light. 'An' when I die,' she had said, 'if you all don' put me in de groun' wit' it, I goin' come an' haunt you, you hear me?'

Now here she was, giving that very ring away with a smile on her face. Her sacrifice made such an impression on me that I felt I could do no less than give up my own tiny silver earrings which another of my mother's clients had so kindly given her some months before. However, not having attained her spiritual maturity, it was with a wistful pang or two that I removed them from my ears and handed them to Brother Caleb. My mother's fond look of pride rewarded me.

'God goin' bless you, Sista Dixon,' said Brother Caleb. 'You an' you man keepin' a fine Christian home an' you bringin' up you chile like a true olive branch.' He picked up his walking stick and rose from the chair, grunting with the effort it required, then shuffled out of the house, saying, 'I gives you good day.'

Nothing more was heard of Thomas Peters through the rest of that spring and summer and into the first weeks of the autumn. In the months following his departure, our lives once more settled into their usual pattern except that in the course of all our church services and prayer meetings, special prayers were offered for his safety and success.

Life in Birchtown hardly changed from day to day, but for me it was pleasant and, in any case, all that I had ever known. I passed my days in cleaning out the house, feeding the chickens, peeling vegetables and doing all the family mending - a task at which I had become skilled. Daniel was responsible to see that we had an unfailing supply of firewood and, in addition, being by nature a quiet and solitary soul, he enjoyed hunting and occasionally went fishing. Thus stews made with fish or from the many small animals he killed featured often in our meals.

Only two events worthy of note took place during those summer months. The first was my baptism in July, for which my mother made me a straight white cotton shift with long wide sleeves. It was the sort of garment I imagined to be the apparel of angels, but I remember that in my growing awareness of becoming a woman, instead of glorying in my salvation I was anxious lest too much of my body be revealed by the clinging wet cloth when I was lifted out of the water. The second major event was the revival service which Pastor George held in Shelburne.

If I were to attempt to choose the most out-standing characteristic of the Birchtown community, it would be our devotion to the Christian religion. A large part of our daily lives was given to devotions and church activities. Small as the community was, there were three separate congregations — Methodists formed the largest group, followed by the Baptists and then the Countess of Huntingdon's Connexion. There was not one day in the week when singing, clapping, praying or preaching was not at some hour to be heard coming from one of the cabins; and we attended long church services twice on Sunday. A revival service was therefore an occasion only the infirm would have missed, so almost the whole of Birchtown turned out on the appointed day. Regardless of denomination, hundreds of people poured into Shelburne to hear Pastor George preach.

I have heard many preachers in my time, but never another to compare with Pastor David George. Sometimes he spoke in ordinary conversational cadences but at other times his voice thundered with such authority that it was as if the Lord himself were once again walking on earth. Sometimes threatening, sometimes cajoling, he used his whole body to convey his message; his hands, his shoulders, his head, his neck, all helped him preach. He himself was often moved to tears, and as for his congregation, grown men moaned and even wept while women often shrieked and groaned as he spoke. I re-member being much affected by his voice even when I was too young to understand a word he was saying.

That summer, the theme of the revival was 'Sin and Repentance', and Pastor George chose for one of his examples the conversion of St Paul. It was a story that lent itself well to the full demonstration of his preaching powers. As usual, he began his sermon quietly and in more formal English than the rest of us could speak:

'Children, today I am going to talk about St. Paul; that man who made himself a whip to chas-tise the Christians living in Jerusalem. That same man, Paul - used to be called Saul at that time - that same man, when he had been saved by the Lamb of God - that same man spread the gospel of Jee-sus throughout the land. No man, no-oth-er-man was as strong in the Lord asPaul. Let me tell you all how it happened.' And so he went on. By the time he arrived at the place in the narra-tive when Paul received his vision on the road to Damascus, the sweat was pouring down his face and he was deep in our familiar dialect. I had read that story of Paul's conversion many, many times, but the way Pastor George said, 'Saul, Saul, why you persecutin' me?' would have moved a heart of stone. His voice brought a rush of tears to my eyes and a sob to my throat, while all around bedlam reigned because, added to the general din caused by the cries and groans of their parents and grandparents were the fright-ened wails of the young children present. It was fortunate that that year the revival was taking place in a large open field just outside Shelburne. On a previous occasion it had been held in the Baptist Chapel and the town marshalls had been sent to disperse the rowdy congregation for disturbing the peace of the white inhabitants. We returned home weak with fatigue but I, for one, was filled with peace and joy.

The summer was always a time of relatively easy living; a time when, bare-footed and bare-headed, I could romp with other children my age in the flower-strewn fields, or dip my toes in the river, lost in dreams. In the summertime my spirit soared free and Mammy often had to scold me for bursting into song in what she considered an unseemly fashion. There were plenty of fruits and vegetables. Small animals abounded in the near-by woods and the ocean teemed with fish. This was the time when koonkings, such as we still organize, used to take place. Every table would be laden with pies, more than one kind of stew, pot roasts, heaps of potatoes, baskets of fruit, cheese and biscuits. The feasting, singing and dancing in a circle would continue until late at night or early in the morning according to your mood and stamina. Bro and Mammy always had to rouse Daniel and me from sleep when the festivities were over for, full to bursting, we could never keep our eyes open so far into the night. By that hour, our parents would be far removed from their usual sober and dignified selves; they would laugh and jest at the tops of their voices all the way home. The drinking of liquor is not frowned upon by our religious leaders so there were always several gallons of ale and other kinds of home-brewed liquor, as well as rum, at these koonkings. It was loudly upheld that not to leave casks empty would invite misfortune, and so the celebration ended only when every container could be turned upside down.

During those balmy days and nights, the many hardships of life in Birchtown assumed a smaller importance. People, older and more far-seeing than I was, may have watched and waited hopefully for the return of Thomas Peters, but except during the regular prayers for him, I never gave his mission more than a fleeting thought. If he had never returned I would have forgotten him altogether. However, return he did and with his coming the course of my life took a direction I could never have imagined.

Chapter 4
The return of Thomas Peters

It was by now mid-September and the joys of the summer would soon be at an end. One afternoon, Daniel returned from a fishing excursion looking more excited than I had ever seen him. He brought the tidings that a visitor had arrived at Pastor Wilkinson's place next door to the Methodist Chapel and, although he had only seen his back, he was convinced from the sound of his voice that the man was Thomas Peters.

'Deannie, he walk like he a king, an' if you hear how he shoutin' out to Daddy Moses — loud an' jolly like he been drinkin' ale.'

'You tink dem English people done answer him good?'

'Yes; I tink he happy 'bout what dey done tell him .. '

'I kin wager anytin' when Bro an' Mammy hear de news dey goin' want to go to Daddy Moses house an' hear everytin' dat done happen,' I said.

Bro had heard the news and had already passed by Pastor Wilkinson's house before coming home; but he had not seen Thomas Peters. He burst into our cabin, exclaiming, 'Deannie, Daniel, wonderful news... wonderful news! Where you Mammy? Thomas Peters done come back an'.

'I done see him, Bro,' Daniel said.

'You done see him? How he look to you ... happy?'

'Very happy Bro.'

'Hallelujah! What I always sayin' to you Mammy?'

'Wait on de Lord,' I answered merrily.

'Yes, indeed! Wait on de Lord. He never goin' fail... Dis night we goin' down de Methodis' Chapel to hear what Thomas Peters have to tell we.'

Mammy was late coming home that evening and somehow or other had not yet heard the glad tidings. She became too excited to touch her food when we told her.

'How you all expect me to eat when my heart jumpin' up and down so!' she said. 'Bro, look at you, chompin' bread like dis a ordinary night ... Make haste, man!'

She refused to remove her coat and paced up and down the small room as we finished our food and prepared to go out.

'Leave de plate; leave de plate,' she said. 'I goin' eat when we come back, den we kin clean up ... Come on now, or else we goin' have to stan' up de whole time again.'

How very different our walk to the Methodist Chapel was from the usual silent journey to attend church services! Mammy kept up a barrage of questions to most of which none of us could provide any answer.

'Patience, Sista,' Bro had to say at last. 'Jus' now we goin' reach de place an' you goin' hear everytin'.'

Several other people were on the Shelburne Road that evening, all bound for the same destination. When we arrived, it was as before exceedingly uncomfortable. In every pew bodies were as squashed as it was possible to be without danger to life. While we awaited the arrival of the hero, it was as hot as if we were close to one of Mammy's boiling wash-pots; and the air was not as fresh.

At last, a whisper began that Pastor Wilkinson had arrived. All heads turned towards the chapel door through which he came limping, led as always by his small grandson; behind him came Thomas Peters. Even by the dim light from the wall sconces, I saw at once what Daniel had remarked on earlier. Thomas Peters was indeed different from the man of our first acquaintance. Dressed in a coat of better cut, in contrast to the shabby garb in which he had first faced us, he was somewhat slimmer than before and walked with a decidedly jaunty tread. The greatest change of all was in his countenance which I can only describe by saying it was as if a lamp had been lit within him.

Sensing everyone's impatience, Pastor Wilkinson said what was, for him, a brief prayer then, before calling upon Thomas Peters to speak, he reminded us of the purpose of his visit to England and hinted that the mission had been successful in a way that showed that the hand of the Lord was truly in the undertaking. At these words, cries of 'Hosanna!', 'Hallelujah!' and 'Praise de Lord' echoed around the chapel, accompanied by loud applause. It was amid this jubilation that Thomas Peters rose to address us for the second time.

'Brodas an' sistas,' he said, 'Yes, indeed, Prai ... ai... se de Lord!... Two time, I done cross de water an' here I is ... safe an' whole ... An' when you hear what I goin' tell you, you goin' shout hallelujah till dey hear you inside heaven.'

Thomas Peters described his arrival in England and how he travelled to London where he met other Negroes. These kind people arranged a lodging for him, then took him to the office of the Secretary of State, where he was allowed to present his petition. A week later, nothing more had happened and he had begun to feel despondent lest his petition had been thrown aside. Then, on the afternoon of the seventh day, an Englishman came to his lodgings, introduced himself as Mr. Granville Sharp and told Thomas Peters that the Secretary of State had shown him the petition. He informed Thomas Peters that he had a proposition for his people in Nova Scotia, but would not disclose it until two other important people had met him. He took Thomas Peters to a mansion and introduced him, to the owner - a Mr. Henry Thornton, and another man, called Sir Thomas Clarkson. They told Thomas Peters that his appearance was a godsend; that they had been fighting against the Slave Trade for many years, and that to further their cause, had started a commercial undertaking on the western coast of Africa where the trade was carried out. Called the Sierra Leone Company, its purpose was to promote wholesome trading with the natives. To that end, they had acquired land from a local king to which, three years previously, they had sent some of the poor Negroes living in England. That attempt to found a colony had failed; they had been concerned that if they could not find new settlers the whole enterprise would collapse, leaving the slave traders triumphant. They proposed that Thomas Peters and his people should travel to this place in the western part of Africa called Sierra Leone and start a new colony. There would be plenty of land for everyone.

Hitherto, the congregation had given Thomas Peters as rapt attention as on his previous visit, but on hearing this proposal, murmurs of discontent began. Mammy looked at Bro, Bro looked at Mammy. One or two people near me snorted in derision. Leave Nova Scotia and go to Africa! Where in this world was that? Thomas Peters held up his hand for silence and, as he continued to speak, people began to realise that the suggestion was not so ridiculous after all; that it was, in fact, worthy of their consideration.

'Brodas an' Sistas, I knows what you all tinkin', but believe me, I say de Lord done answer we. I tink he workin' in dem English people. Mine, I knows de tin' dey askin' goin' be hard to do. De place far from here... Don' know where exac'ly; we got to cross water ... But as for me, after I talk to dem, I done make up my mine to go; an' I goin' tell you why ... Di ol' folk on my plantation been tell we dat Africa de place darkies use to live befo' whitefolk buy dem or catch dem an' bring den to America to be slave. Africa de place God made for we darkies; Africa in our blood. In Englan' dey tell me de weder nice an' warm dere; ... an' I goin' get de farm I been waitin' for all dis time... I got notin' to keep me here ...Notin'... Africa de proper home for darkies an' Thomas Peters goin' home!...Is all I have to say, good people. I leavin' you all to ponder de matter. Ponder it deep. Notin' done settle yet. Pray 'bout it! I knows some people not sufferin' like some. I knows some goin' say, even if dey sufferin', dey done use 'Scotia now an' dey not goin' move to no strange country again. I kin understan' dat; but if, like me, you got notin', den you got notin' to lose if you go. ... Right dis minute as I standin' here talkin', Sir Thomas Clarkson broda, lefnant John Clarkson done reach 'Scotia'. He in Halifax now. When he finish he business dere he comin' to Shelburne. He goin' tell you more 'bout de place an' what dis company dey done make plannin' for we if we 'gree to go. He goin' answer everytin' you want to know. Is after, dat he goin' ask you to make up you mine... Is all I kin say for now, but befo' I take my seat, I want to bless you all for de money you been give me. I been go to Englan' like a proper man, not like a beggar. I knows you all been make plenty sacrifice to give me de money. God Bless You!'

Thomas Peters seated himself amid applause that threatened to shake the rafters of the chapel and there began such a clamour of voices that Pastor Wilkinson asked us to remember that we were still in the Lord's house and not at the fisherman's wharf in Shelburne. To remind us further, he made us rise and sing a doxology, which, as usual, we did at the tops of our voices:

'Praise God from whom all blessings flow
Praise him all creatures here below;
Praise him above, ye heavenly host;
Praise Father, Son and Holy Ghost.'

By the time he pronounced the Benediction, a certain calm had been restored though, as on the previous occasion, many people surged forward to shake Thomas Peters by the hand and slap him on the back in admiration.

On the way home, neighbours of ours, Brother Scipio Conley and his wife, walked with my parents. Several paces behind them Daniel walked beside me, deep in his private thoughts as was his wont. I could not keep my thoughts to myself and interrupted his own.

'Danny, if you been by youself ... no Bro, no Mammy to ask, you 'gree to go' to Africa?'

'I be de firs' one to put my name in de book when de Englishman come,' Danny said. 'True?' I said. 'Me, I 'fraid Danny ... Crossin' de water all dat way ... Supposin' de ship go down an' ... an' dem shark come an' crunch me all up.'

The very thought of my body being reduced to fragments of bone and scraps of bloody flesh was enough to make me shudder. Daniel laughed aloud, nudging me away.

'Deannie, you too foolish; when you goin' grow up? Every day ship crossin' de water. Every day. Look Thomas Peters. He been go an' he done come back all in one piece ... Anyway, is Bro an' Mammy got to say, if we goin'. Maybe dey goin' say we better to stay right here.'

'Anh, Anh, maybe Bro, but not Mammy,' I said with the utmost certainty. 'I spyin' her face when Thomas Peters talkin', an' after he finish she look jus' like how he been look - all light up inside ... An' you know how she always complain an' complain when de weather turn col'. I wager you anytin', Mammy goin' make Bro put he name down even if he don' want to go.'

Chapter 5
We meet Lieutenant John Clarkson and Bro decides

Our neighbours parted company from Bro and Mammy when they reached their cabin and, as I had predicted, my mother straightaway began her campaign to convince Bro that we should all avail ourselves of the opportunity being offered. In the darkness, and because we were several paces behind them, we could not see them very clearly, nor could we hear their words plainly; but we could detect the note of urgency and conviction in Mammy's voice, and we could make out her jerking head and emphatic gestures. Daniel and I caught up with them as we reached the path leading to our cabin - just in time to hear her bring out one of the arguments I had known she would use.

'Bro, no more winter! You tink I want to spend all my life pickin' washin' dat ice done make stiff like board an' ... an' goin' from dis place to Shelburne when my toe an' my finger ready to fall off wit' de chilblain an' my breath like smoke when it come from my mout'? ... Bro! How you kin say you not sure yet?'

'Mammy, I not sure yet,' Bro said in a stubborn voice. 'You want for me to say, jus' like dat, we goin' pack up an' leave Scotia? Me an' you managin' jus' fine here. We gettin' food to eat — I workin' reglar, you workin' reglar; Daniel goin' start to bring in sometin' jus' now.'

'Bro, listen ... If we go, we goin' be able to make we lifejus' like how we want ... God givin' us dis chance. I feel it inside of me; an' I want de chance for Danny an' for Deannie. What kine life dey goin' get here, eh? You tell me dat.'

Thus the argument raged in our home and no doubt in other homes wherever Thomas Peters spoke to communities of Negroes in Nova Scotia.

Mammy never missed an opportunity to assail Bro's resistance; I was at once amazed and amused at the variety of arguments with which she pressed him. One evening we were eating a stew made of turnips and she said in a cajoling voice.

'Bro, if we go to Africa we kin plant all dem tin' you like to eat in Car'lina - rice, yam, sweet potato - you 'member my sweet potato pie, hm? You not tired wit' eatin' turnip an' white potato every day?'

Bro replied with a straight face, 'An' you not 'fraid of snake no more, eh?'

'Snake!' Mammy dismissed them with a wave of her hand. 'I done live wit' snake in Car'lina an' no snake not goin' stop me livin' in Africa.'

On another occasion she produced this argument:

'Bro, when we go to Africa we kin stop to worry 'bout dem people who want to catch we an' sell we again.'

'You done forget Africa is where dey been catch you grandaddy an' bring him to America, eh?' Bro retorted.

'But dat Sierra Leone Company goin' protect we.'

Bro grunted, unimpressed. He proved surprisingly obstinate. It was only gradually, and with the strong support of Daniel, for once outspoken, that Mammy wore away his resistance to the extent that he began to say, 'If we go to Africa.'

Mr. John Clarkson arrived in Shelburne towards the end of October and word went around that he would be visiting Birchtown shortly to meet all interested persons in the Methodist Chapel. He arrived on a Sunday afternoon and that evening, in spite of the weather which was most dreary, being rainy and cold, a crowd of at least five hundred people assembled to listen to him. To the surprise and annoyance of all, the first white man introduced was not Mr. Clarkson but one Lieutenant Miller who was seeking recruits for military service in the West Indies. He droned on and on, and was listened to with barely suppressed impatience. Not a single hand went up when he asked for volunteers, so he went his way. Since Pastor Wilkinson was indisposed that day, it was his assistant, Pastor Luke Jordan, who introduced Mr. Clarkson and invited him to mount the pulpit.

It was plain from Mr. Clarkson's very first words that here was one white man who possessed genuine feelings of sympathy towards our race. His sense of mission lit up his whole countenance and he spoke with such earnestness that it was surely the man rather than his words that convinced some who had been but half - persuaded when they entered the church. In spite of his youthful and somewhat frail appearance, I soon believed that I could trust Mr. Clarkson with my life; that I could safely follow him to the ends of the earth.

He described the Sierra Leone Company's land in Africa as being not unlike Shelburne, with the same closeness to the ocean, though some three thousand miles distant, and in a hot climate. He warned us that life there would not be easy at the beginning because, though the country was blessed with plenty of warmth and sunshine, there was heavy rainfall for four months together, every single year. He said that those who were comfortable in Nova Scotia should hesitate before leaving certainty for an uncertain future, but assured those prepared to take a chance that he was convinced Sierra Leone had much to offer that was good. He said any land we received would be given free of all cost to ourselves and that the only rates and taxes we might be charged would be used to improve our situation and provide such benefits as schools and hospitals. I was struck by this white man who seemed so sincere in his wish to improve the lot of a people with whom he had no other tie than that of Christian charity.

When he finished speaking, people hurled questions at him from all sides. As a result of the onslaught, we learned that the journey to Africa would take about fifty days, that transportation would be provided at the expense of the Sierra Leone Company, that an agent had already been appointed to secure contracts for the necessary ships and provisions, and that the Company would send officials ahead of us to prepare for our arrival. We learned that provisions would be sold to us at a cheap rate, or on credit, until our own farms produced crops, that we would be provided with all the tools necessary for their cultivation, and that everyone, both white and black, would be equal under British Law.

The only stern note in Mr. Clarkson's voice came at the end of the questioning when he informed us that the Company sought only honest, sober and industrious settlers, and that he would accept no applications from people who could not provide testimonials of good character and proof that they were free from debt. On hearing this, many people looked at each other in dismay. Mammy asked in an undertone,

'Bro, what we goin' do if Mr Fowlis refuse to give you a testimonial?'

'Leave off you worryin',' Bro muttered. 'Who been say I goin' ask him, anyhow?' Whereupon, Mammy gave him a look of exasperation. Indeed, he kept us in suspense as to his intentions for another week; not until the following Sunday did he finally announce his decision to go to Africa.

It had been an exceptionally cold day for the time of year, with the early afternoon sky the eerie mustard colour that gave warning of a snow storm. It was unusual for such a sky to appear before the autumn was over. We had said our evening prayers and were about to retire for the night. As head of the household, Bro was always the last to visit the privy in the backyard. Like the rest of us had been, he was shivering from the cold when he returned; but unlike us he had a thick coating of snow on his head and shoulders.

'Mammy, Daniel, Deannie...'We sensed great excitement as he removed his coat and shook away the snow, 'Tomorrow I goin' put down we name to go to Africa.'

Mammy, Daniel and I exchanged mystified glances, for in the end, his decision seemed to have come out of the blue. However, this was not the case, as he went on to explain.

'All dis time you all been tryin' to force me to say yes 'bout goin' to Africa, I been prayin' hard an' I done beg de Lord to show me a sign to know what I mus' do. I done beg an' beg, an' tonight, jus' now, de Lord done answer me. See dis snow? Dis snow de sign I been waitin' for.'

With a look of deep elation such as we had never seen before, he raised his hands and eyes towards heaven, exclaiming, 'I tank you, Jesus! Tank you; tank you.' Since neither Mammy, nor Daniel nor I were altogether enlightened by his words, Mammy said, 'What you mean, Bro?'

'Dis early snow a message from de Lord,' he answered. 'He tellin' me de winter comin' goin' be very hard; dere goin' be plenty sufferin' here; maybe no food to eat even. De Lord tellin'me to take my family an' go.'

'Hallelujah!' Mammy cried. She brushed away snowflakes still clinging to Bro's hair, then embraced him with all her might.

'Mammy!' Bro said, pretending to be shocked by her behaviour. ' Such foolishness on de Lord's Day!'

Showing no repentance, Mammy continued to hold him close. In the end, he wrapped his own arms around her and for a moment they swayed together. Full of glad relief that the matter was settled at last, and greatly amused by this unwonted display of affection between our parents, Daniel and I chortled as we readied our pallets for the night.

Chapter 6
We prepare to leave Nova Scotia for- ever

I have come to believe that when it is a matter of a certain kind of cunning and the ability to manipulate people for their own ends, the Englishman must be without equal. It transpired that my mother had been right to be concerned about the problems people might face when trying to obtain testimonials from their employers. With his own attitude of Christian charity to all, Mr. Clarkson did not take into account the possibility of malice on the part of his kinfolk in Nova Scotia. Many of them had benefited from having in their midst hundreds of Negroes desperate for a work, and in the weeks following Mr. Clarkson's visit, they did their utmost to prevent a general exodus of this cheap source of labour. Hardly a day went by without the Birchtown community seething from news of their mischief-making.

Some employers demanded that our people produce certificates proving that they were freemen and not runaway slaves - a possibility that had caused them no concern before. Many of our people had been in Nova Scotia since the end of the war between England and the Americans; some of them had lost their certificates while others had handled them so often or so carelessly that they had become stained and tattered and barely legible. When such was the case, their employers refused to give them the benefit of the doubt and there the matter ended. Other employers, equally without scruples, were said to take advantage of their servants' lack of book learning and gave them testimonials full of damaging lies. True to his warning, Mr. Clarkson and his agents rejected such applications outright, no matter how passionately the allegations were denied. Other employers produced false documents to prove that certain individuals were indebted to them. Mr. Clarkson and his agents rejected those also. The lengths to which those wicked employers went were both astonishing and alarming. Fortunately, after a time, Mr. Clarkson and his agents became suspicious of the large number of bad debtors and thieves among the applicants and decided to rely on their own judgment after personal interviews.

An atmosphere of uncertainty and suspicion, greatly disturbed the peace of Birchtown during those weeks. To make the situation worse, printed leaflets began to appear, pushed under cabin doors at night, pinned to the chapel doors, or simply scattered about the place. They warned all seeking to leave Nova Scotia that Sierra Leone was a land notorious for its unhealthy climate, and that the natives were savages known to be hostile to foreigners. Many people who had registered for the journey lost courage at the possibility of an early death and withdrew their names, though not as great a number as might have been expected to do so. Some of our own people also campaigned against the planned expedition. In Birchtown they went so far as to draw up a petition calling those who had decided to go to Africa a bunch of fools; many heads of families signed it. Bitterness against the government grew stronger; as rumours went round that the authorities were behind the attempts to prevent our departure.

However, while we were eating our meal one evening, Mammy told us that her client, Mrs. Catchpole, had assured her that the Governor and his Council were playing no part in the shameful trickery and deception. Apparently, her husband had a friend in Halifax who knew one of the members of the Council and was therefore kept well informed on such matters. She told Mammy that Governor Parr was giving every possible assistance to Mr. Clarkson and his agents because Thomas Peters's journey to London and the petition he had presented had caused the government great embarrassment. He was only too relieved that the problems caused by our presence in Nova Scotia would soon lessen.

'She beg me not to blame her brodas for how day behavin' to we,' Mammy said. 'She say dey only 'fraid Mr. Clarkson goin' take away all de honest, sober, hard - workin' darkies an' leave all de useless one, an' de one who always causin' trouble to be millstone roun' dey neck.'

Bro gave an angry snort. 'What you Mrs. Catchpole think when she tell you dat, hmm? She tink we goin' be sorry for dem an' stay here? Whitefolk jus' plain selfish. Dey tryin' to spoil we chance for better life so dey kin enjoy easy livin'.'

'Ah, Bro! Mrs. Catchpole not like dat,' Mammy said in mild reproach. 'Look how she help we in de famine time. She a good soul; she only tryin' for me to understan' how dem oda white folk feelin'.'

'Mammy, don' let's talk 'bout dis tin' again. You vexin' me more an' more. All dis time when we been sufferin', when day treatin' we like dog instead of people, dey been care how we feelin'? I don' like to hear nonsense! ... An' de tin' dat make my blood boil is how some of we own people so stupid, dey helpin' dem to spoil dis chance we got now!'

Bro's anger was typical of the prevailing mood in Birchtown and Shelburne. Quarrels broke out within families; old friends stopped talking to each other as those who wanted to go to Africa argued with those who either had always believed, or had been persuaded, that it was a foolhardy venture. I remember it as a disagreeable and unsettling time; only my parents' confidence helped to give me a sense of security. On more than one occasion, Bro said, 'All I knows is, if de Lord done give a sign an' you don' obey, you goin' be sorry. '

The situation changed all of a sudden early in December. Once again, an old rumour swept through the lanes and cabins of Birchtown with the speed of a forest fire. It was whispered with great agitation that white men had been seen seizing young Negroes in Shelburne to sell to West Indian plantations. Whether this old rumour was part of another clever ploy I cannot say, but it could hardly have surfaced at a more opportune moment. The panic it caused swelled the number of applicants for emigration to Africa.

Meanwhile, my own family's plans to leave Nova Scotia continued to proceed without hindrance. Not only did Bro receive a favourable testimonial from Mr. Fowlis; that generous man also gave him a bonus on his wage. One or two of my mother's clients gave her the cold shoulder when she announced her intention to leave Nova Scotia, but the others, led by Mrs. Catchpole, took the news kindly and, as the days went by, became as excited as Mammy herself.

Each adult male member of the expedition was allowed two tons of luggage, every female one ton, and every child half a ton. Our poor furnishings and few clothes could scarcely have amounted to one ton but for those kind white ladies. They gave us so many old clothes, pots, pans, chairs and tables that Daniel and I had to accompany Mammy on her journeys to deliver and collect laundry in order to help her bring the gifts home. In the end Bro was obliged to borrow a wagon from Mr. Fowlis to convey the remainder of the items to Birchtown.

Mammy and I now became busy with our needles, altering our hand-me-downs. By the time we finished our work, she possessed three good dresses and three for everyday wear, I possessed the same number, while Daniel and my father were outfitted with two pairs of working trousers each, a sturdy jacket, two pairs of breeches and several shirts. We were even fortunate with footwear, although a perfect fit was impossible to achieve.

By the middle of November, winter had truly settled in - a winter as harsh and as bitter as Bro had been warned to expect. One morning, high snowdrifts jammed shut the door to our cabin so that Daniel had to climb through a window to dig out a pathway to it. We were eager to be gone. Despite the severe cold, preparations for our departure proceeded apace with the noise of hammers on wood ringing out hour after hour. Since Bro could no longer work in the open, Mammy abandoned her trade and he converted the shed where she had been accustomed to do the washing during the winter months into a carpentry workshop. He and Daniel made packing cases not only for our family, but for others not fortunate enough to have their skills. Bro also arranged to sell our plot and cabin to a Colonel Bluck - one of the few Negroes in Birchtown and Shelburne to enjoy a good measure of prosperity. Finally, Mammy insisted that we all go to Shelburne to thank Mrs. Catchpole and her friends for their gifts. That mission accomplished, the Dixon family was ready to undertake the journey into the unknown.

I had not entirely succeeded in putting away my fears about a long sea voyage, but being caught up in the excitement of preparation, had been too busy to dwell much upon them. However, as the time of our departure drew nearer I discovered that, fears aside, the pulling up of roots can never be accomplished without a measure of pain. It saddened me to realise that I would soon leave behind much of what I had loved and taken for granted in Birchtown. How I would miss the resinous odour of wood smoke mixed with frosty winter air! Would I ever again catch my breath at a sight to compare with the blazing red and gold and brown of maple leaves in the autumn of the year? Would there be flower-strewn fields in which I could safely frolic? With all that we had lacked in comfort and ease, Birchtown had been my home for many a year. Could this unknown land in Africa ever become as much a home to me? God only knew. The whole of Birchtown's Baptist congregation was joining the exodus and others must have shared my anxieties, for it was my impression that prayers at the meeting-house were more fervent than ever before.

In those last days when the packing was done and all we had to do was wait for our summons, I sometimes surprised a brooding expression on Bro's face which made me know that he also was wondering what the future held in store; wondering what manner of unforeseen trials and dangers might be awaiting us in a strange land. During those last days in Birchtown, whenever he called upon Daniel or me to read aloud from the Bible, he asked for one of the psalms, and made us repeat certain verses as if he needed to strengthen his faith that all would be well. Not so Mammy; she seemed to be facing the future with a fearless optimism that Sierra Leone held the answer to all her longings and her prayers. She bustled about our cabin, talking, laughing, more merry altogether than I had ever known her to be.

Our marching orders came at the very end of that year, by which time we were all but consumed by our impatience. We were told to proceed in two days' time to Shelburne, there to embark on the vessels which had been hired to transport the emigrants from that area to the port of Halifax where all members of the expedition were to assemble.

Chapter 7
Waiting to depart

Before dawn on the second day of the New Year, four hundred Negroes left Birchtown, Nova Scotia, never to return. Wagons and carts had been hired to transport our luggage; as they began to roll down the Shelburne road that icy morning we said our farewells forever, and many were the tearful scenes.

The embarkation took the best part of that day and, trembling from cold, weariness and hunger, I thought that the confusion of worn out furniture, battered trunks and massive cases would never be sorted out. However, as if by a miracle, we were all settled on board by the late afternoon and set sail at first light the next morning.

Our arrival at Halifax was for me a time of almost unbearable excitement, for the scene that met my astonished gaze was beyond any previous experience. The vast harbour seemed to stretch for miles yet, even so, appeared to be chock - full of vessels of every description: majestic three-masted ships, small single-masted craft, clumsy fishing boats, and dinghies bobbing like the playful offspring of the larger vessels. On the wharves and decks, broad-shouldered dock-hands, black as well as white, mingled freezing breath with the wisps of fog wrapped round the warehouses and masts like ghostly shawls. There was much movement to and fro; profanities and obscene oaths yelled with such abandon that

Mammy shook her head in strong disapproval, saying, 'Chile, lock you ears!' It was only with difficulty that the captain of our ship was able to find a berth, and the day was well advanced before we could disembark.

Never before had I seen such a throng of black people as I beheld on that day. Only the occasions of the revival meetings in Shelburne could be said to approach that number. The menfolk were assisting with the loading, while many huddling groups of women and children stood about the docks wrapped in shawls, blankets, cloaks or men's coats, with all manner of protective covering for their heads and ears. They stamped their feet and beat their shoulders against the bitter cold. Beggars accosted us several times as we threaded our way through the crowd. They were dressed in as queer an assortment of rags as it was possible to imagine - some with one shoe and one boot, men in ladies' winter bonnets, even in ladies' gowns, others with nothing but the shreds of garments to protect them from the biting winds. They were a sorry sight as they limped along, barely strong enough to put one foot before the other, yet afraid to stand still lest they freeze to death in the snow. Whether it was coming face to face with people without hope when I was moving towards a better future, or whether it was that, with increasing years, I was becoming more sensitive to the misfortunes of others, for the first time in my life I felt somewhat guilty, as if I were in some way responsible for their plight. And I could not escape the thought that they would have done well to return to their masters before becoming so wretched. However, knowing Mammy's opinion of such a cowardly sentiments, I was glad that she could not read my mind. She would surely have said, 'Yes, dey sufferin', an' maybe dey goin' die, but dey goin' die free.'

One of the Company's agents met us on the wharf - a stocky, red-faced individual whose calves bulged sturdily below grey breeches. In a gruff manner, he demanded to know whether we were the folk from Birchtown and when we gave him an affirmative answer, said that all of the Baptist denomination should enter a warehouse two hundred yards or so along the quay. We did as told and were surprised to find, already established there, Pastor George and those of his Shelburne flock who had decided to join the exodus to Sierra Leone. Also awaiting us inside was another Company agent with a brisk, high-pitched voice. He gave everyone two blankets, a tin cup, and a plate and spoon which he said we could take to Africa. He then divided us into groups of several families each and appointed a leader, named 'Captain', from among the men. We found ourselves in the group headed by Pastor George. It consisted of only twenty small families because, said the agent, we would be on the ship, Lucretia, with Mr. Clarkson. Having instructed every able-bodied man to be present on the quay the next day to assist in the loading of the transports, he called for volunteers from among the women to undertake the preparation of meals. Mammy was one of the first to come forward, and did so dragging me along. In the end, ten women offered their services as cooks, which seemed to satisfy the agent. He announced that our provisions for the day would be brought to our lodging every morning.

'I believe that's all for now folks,' he said in conclusion. 'We have done our best for you, but you goin' be a mite uncomfortable till all parties have arrived and the transports are loaded.'

That agent spoke the truth when he warned that we should expect discomfort in our temporary lodgings. The warehouse was one immense room with a high roof and a stone floor— bare except for a number of large braziers and a pile of roughly made pallets which, when not in use as beds or seats, were stacked around the walls. The only warmth came from the braziers on which meals were prepared and, in spite of the fact that there were several of them, in that vast space the heat they gave off seemed hardly to affect the freezing temperature. Every night the 'Captains' decided which families could sleep near the braziers; everyone else had to make do with their blankets and the warmth provided by bodies lying close together. Nothing but the sketchiest ablutions took place in the mornings, for no one willingly exposed bare skin except for hands and faces; besides, each person received just one cup of water a day for that purpose. As was to be expected under such harsh conditions, several among our number came down with chills and fever so that the silence of the night was often broken by groans and hacking coughs. However, faith and hope kept our spirits high. Mammy, and other women of her age, strengthened both by singing lively hymns as they worked and waited. They encouraged us all to join in, declaring that pastime to be as warming to the blood as a tot of hard liquor.

The food supplied was plain, but we were accustomed to plain fare, and in those temperatures, all one needed was a warm lining for the stomach. That was provided by a breakfast of boiled oats or cornmeal, mixed with molasses or maple syrup. At midday, the hot meal consisted of salt fish or salt pork stewed with white potatoes, dried peas or turnips, and in the evenings, we washed down a piece of coarse bread with a cupful of thin soup. Those meals were typical of the fare that would sustain us through the long weeks at sea.

During the intervals between preparing one meal and the next, time sometimes hung so heavily on our hands that Mammy and I were driven to venture out of our warehouse home and brave the snow. We either went down to the docks to join people watching the loading of the transports, or else wandered into Halifax town. One afternoon we climbed halfway to the top of Citadel Hill, upon which stood the army barracks, and enjoyed the view over the entire harbour. It was on our return journey, when we were but a few hundred yards from our temporary home, that we encountered Felicia Porter.

My first sight of her was of a solitary figure hurrying towards us with head bowed. She was hugging herself in protection against the wind. As she came abreast of us, she instinctively raised her head and I saw that she was a Negro like ourselves, though light-skinned, and that she was young, though older than I. Her frail appearance immediately roused Mammy's motherly instincts and she stopped her, saying,

'Girl, where you goin', walkin' by youself in dis town wit' all dem no-good riff-raff 'bout de place. You from roun' dis part?'

'No, Mam, I from Saint John,' the girl answered in a low shaking voice. 'I goin' to Africa wit' my broda ... We only waitin' let de boat be ready.'

Hardly noticing from whence she said she had come, I exclaimed, 'We goin' to Africa too!'

As if I had not spoken, Mammy said, 'You from Saint John?... I done hear tell dat place far from dis part ... Come walk wit' we a while;... Too col' to stan' an' talk.' 'Yes, Mam, Saint John far from here,'the girl answered, adding with a proud lift to her shoulders, 'An' me an' my broda, we walk all de way.'

That more astonishing information stopped Mammy in her tracks.

'You done what?' she said. 'You tellin' me you walk all de way from Saint John to Halifax when de place freezin' so! How come you folks 'gree to dat?'

'Don' know where in dis worl' my folks be, Mam,' the girl said. 'My broad, Junius, de only famly I got.'

By this time we had reached the warehouse; Mammy said, 'Is here we lodgin' ... You lodgin' far from here?'

'Not too far, Mam; ... up barrack way.'

'Come inside a while an' warm yourself some. My man goin' come back jus' now; he or my boy, Daniel, goin' walk wit' you to you lodgin', you hear?... Dis place not safe at all ... Look, foolish me, all dis talkin' an' askin ' question an' I not even ask you name. What dey call you, chile?'

'Felicia, Mam ... Felicia Porter, but mos' everybody call me Licia.'

'Dat a pretty name for a fine girl. My name Rebecca Dixon, but you jus' call me Mammy like everybody do; an' dis my girl, Deannie.'

Felicia and I exchanged wide smiles, ours being a case of instant affection.

Once inside the warehouse, Mammy called out. 'You all come listen to dis brave girl who done walk all de way from Saint John to here.'

The response to her invitation was immediate, for any diversion was welcome. Felicia told a rapt audience gathered round one of the braziers, that she and her brother, Junius, were the freeborn children of a mulatto woman, known as Louisa Porter. She abandoned them when Felicia was twelve and her brother, eleven years old. The orphans, for they had known no father, were forced to become indentured servants, bound for seven years to an innkeeper - a Mr. Cooper, whose tavern was a mile or so outside Saint John. The seven years were almost over and their employer had threatened that if they did not bind themselves for a further seven years, he would sell them to a plantation in the West Indies. The siblings were in a quandary, for they had endured hell on earth with the innkeeper - sleeping in the stable, and suffering beatings and vicious kicks, his wife feeding them only just enough to maintain their strength for ceaseless labour. In the circumstances they dreaded the prospect of continuing at the inn, yet thought the alternative even worse. They had all but reached a state of despair when the Lord took charge of their affairs - at least, the women listening declared it to be the work of the Lord (I doubt whether at that time, either Felicia or Junius had any inkling of the ways of the Lord).

From time to time, their employer suffered badly from the gout. About the middle of the month of October, felled by another attack, he sent Junius Porter to fetch an apothecary from Saint John. It was there that Junius met another Negro - a Richard Crankapone who expressed surprise that he had not left to join the expedition.

'What expedition you talkin' 'bout?' Junius had asked and Richard Crankapone explained that he was talking about an expedition to a place where freed Negroes would be given land and become their own masters. He had himself learnt about it quite by chance and was on his way to add his name to the register. Immediately seeing a way out of their predicament, Junius Porter joined Richard Crankapone, only to discover on arrival at the place of registration that it had ended and the last of the transports had departed for Halifax. Fortunately, their informants were able to tell them that the expedition would not sail until the New Year.

It did not take the young men long to decide to try to reach Halifax by some means or other. They decided to make their departure that very night and agreed upon a meeting place. Returning late from his errand, Junius Porter only escaped another vicious kick because his master was laid low by his affliction. Curses he received aplenty but those, like water off a duck's back, affected him but little. As planned, he and Felicia crept out of the innkeeper's house that night. Knowing that they would never return, they broke into the larder and stole as much food as they could carry; they also took the thickest blankets they could find in Mrs. Cooper's linen store.

I could not stop gazing at Felicia as she continued to speak, so deeply did her bravery impress me; and her story touched me all the more for being quietly told. She described a nightmarish journey; for the first few miles, the fear that they would be caught stalked them hour by hour.

Winter found them still on the road, their only shelter found in icy barns, their only source of heat the closeness of their own bodies. Once they had exhausted their little store of stolen food, raw potatoes and whatever else they could obtain by begging or stealing formed their only source of nourishment. They had trudged through, or rather, staggered through miles of snow with only rag bandages to keep their toes from frost-bite. How they survived their ordeal was one of God's mysteries, but survive they did and reached Halifax in time to join the expedition.

When she stopped speaking Mammy put a loving arm around her.

'All I kin say is, "What God hath wrought!" ... but I praisin' you too, mine. You look like one puff of breeze goin' carry you off, but you strong as a horse inside ... An' you brave.'

'Where you brother an' de oda man now?' another woman asked.

'Dey done join de loadin', Mam,' Felicia replied. 'Mr Clarkson been say let dem res' till is time to go, but de two of dem got bone ears; dey only res' for two day ... Dey use' to hard livin',' she added with a shrug.

'An' which ship you goin' on?' asked someone else. Felicia smiled broadly and at once her pinched face took on a radiant beauty. 'One dey call Felicity, Mam.' 'See!' Mammy said with a wide triumphant smile, 'De spirit of de Lord still movin'. Is a good sign for you, chile. You name Felicia an' you goin' wit' a ship name Felicity. Look like everytin' goin' be good for you from now on!'

'Amen,' said someone else in the group surrounding Felicia Porter.

We became as fond of each other as if we had been born sisters, but that was in the future. When the men returned, Daniel agreed to escort her to her lodging, albeit reluctantly, since he was bone weary and famished as well. I did not meet Felicia again until we arrived in Sierra Leone, for the next day came word that all was ready for the journey to Africa and we were to prepare to board our transports.

Chapter 8
We set sail

It was the morning of the twelfth day of January, seventeen hundred and ninety-two, and once again we were packed and ready to travel. Looking more red-faced than ever, our agent of the bulging calves arrived at the warehouse, carrying a sheaf of papers. The poor man must have been as anxious as we were for the ships to set sail, for in a manner even gruffer than before, he asked that all heads of families form a queue in front of him; each person was to announce his name when he reached the top. The agent then looked through the sheaf of papers, selected the appropriate one and handed it over. It was a kind of certificate.

'What it say, Dan?' Bro asked when he had received his own. I looked over Daniel's shoulder as he read it out: Bro was entitled to twenty acres of land, Mammy would receive ten acres and Daniel and I five acres each.

'Hear dat, Mammy?' Bro said, elated. 'We goin' get plenty lan' over dere...'

'But forty acre!' Mammy said in disbelief. 'You tink day goin' be able to give we all dat much?'

'If dey don' keep dey promise dis time, de Lord never goin' forgive dem,' Bro answered as if that should be enough to dispel Mammy's anxiety.

The matter of the certificates completed, we left the warehouse without regret - a stream of shivering humanity, clutching blankets and bundles. It was plain to see that some among our party had become so ill that it was doubtful they would reach Africa alive. Yet, there was no question of leaving them behind at that late stage. Each one would have to trust in God and take his chances. Tears of sympathy stung my eyes, for many of them were weeping.

Down at the wharf, we joined other groups of the expedition, all burdened as we were. There seemed to be several hundred of us (I later learned that nearly one thousand and two hundred people sailed from Halifax), but it was an orderly embarkation. Each 'Captain' had been told beforehand which ship to board and the nearest jetty to its berth, which was a good thing on account of the press of people on the quay that morning. Mingled with the throng of passengers were many citizens of Halifax who must have come to the harbour out of curiosity. When we passed one group of men of an uncouth appearance, I distinctly heard one say to another, 'Good riddance. Rowdy folk always dancin', an' singin', an' carryin' on like clowns.'

Mammy also heard those insulting remarks. Knowing that she would shortly be free of the fear of any white man's vengeance, she stopped, turned around and with all the contempt she could put in her voice, said just one word.

'Trash!' The man turned purple. I held my breath, thinking he might strike Mammy; but he only glared at her for a moment, spat at her feet and turned his back on her, muttering an oath as the agent called out,

'Come along, if you please, come along.'

Mammy directed a scornful laugh at the man, and we walked on.

Since our ship, the *Lucretia*, was at anchor some hundred yards or more from the shore, we were obliged to embark from a boat. Climbing up a rope ladder into a rolling vessel from a tossing boat was an experience I hope never to repeat in this life. It brought my heart to my throat, so great was my terror; it was all I could do to force my trembling legs upward. Mammy climbed after me; I could hear her muttering, 'Lord have mercy, Lord have mercy, Lord have Mercy,' with every upward step. It was unthinkable that the sick and infirm should attempt the perilous climb; indeed, they were hoisted up in large contraptions resembling wicker baskets. All this took several hours, but, at last, the seemingly impossible had been accomplished and everyone was safely aboard. Each family was given a parcel of clothes, then required to go below deck to the sleeping quarters, men to one side of the vessel, women and children to the other. By a strange circumstance, I found myself the only person of my age on board the *Lucretia*, thrust among grown women and children of various ages.

The next morning, wrapped in our warmest garments, we assembled on deck, to await the arrival of Mr. Clarkson. It was with dismay that we watched him being hoisted up in a wicker basket, and when he stood before us the reason was plain to see. The strenuous weeks of hasty preparation must have taken their toll on his health, for he looked extremely unwell, with eyes unnaturally bright, and sunken, sallow cheeks. However, he still managed to speak, with something like his old vigour, words to this effect:

'Friends, tomorrow we set out on our great adventure. I beseech you, make this voyage one of peace and harmony as befits Christian brothers and sisters; we shall have enough hardships to face without adding disturbances over petty grievances. I know that will not be easy in our present circumstances, but with patience and forbearance, it can be achieved. Pray, remember that I have been your friend from the beginning. I give you my word that I shall remain so to the end. Whatever you have to bear during the next weeks shall be my burden also. God has been with us thus far, and I trust He shall not fail us now; but neither must we fail Him. I ask you to endeavour to speak quietly at all times, to pay special attention to cleanliness of person, and to attend divine worship. Above all, and I must emphasise this, have no dealings with the sailors ... I now call on our second 'Captain', Pastor George to lead us in prayer.'

Speaking with his usual authority, Pastor George said a lengthy prayer in which he mentioned those who had decided not to join us, the Captain of the *Lucretia,* the crew, the shipbuilders, and the Sierra Leone Company. He also prayed with special fervour for Mr. Clarkson, that he should speedily be restored to health. The temperature on the deck was freezing; my ears and cheeks felt as if they were on fire and I had to clench my jaws to stop my teeth from chattering. I am certain that I did not merely imagine that when Pastor George at last announced the Lord's Prayer, everyone mumbled the words with irreverent haste. We did not sail the next day or the next, for there was not a whisper of wind. But on the fifteenth day of January, all seemed set fair for the voyage to begin.

It was one of those frosty winter mornings of breathtaking beauty, the sky a clear, luminous blue. I looked towards the shore. After the hustle and bustle of the previous days, the harbour was now all but deserted. The few people about were, in all probability, the local agents, or those always captivated by the sight of ships about to set sail. There may also have been a few people present who came to wish us Godspeed. By contrast, the decks of all the ships I could see were crammed with people. Amid much signalling with flags from one ship to the next, we heard a tremendous grating and clanking noise; it was the great iron anchors being raised.

'You all, look!' I shouted, gasping with excitement. The sails of first one ship then another caught the breeze, flapped a few times, then billowed gracefully. From one of the other ships came the faint sound of voices raised in song. The sound grew louder and louder as people on every other ship of the expedition caught the melody and added their own voices to a psalm with which every congregation was familiar.

'God is our refuge and strength, a very present help in trouble. Therefore will we not fear though the earth be removed and though the mountains be carried into the midst of the sea; though the waters thereof roar and be troubled ... The Lord of Hosts is with us; the God of Jacob is our refuge.'

Despite the biting cold, heat suffused my body. My scalp tingled. My knees trembled. My eyes misted over. As I blinked the tears away, I saw that even Danny, usually so self-possessed, was wiping his cheeks. Bro was on his knees, his eyes raised towards heaven, and as for Mammy! She was swaying as she sang, with her arms wrapped about her body. Her eyes tightly shut and her cheeks awash with tears, she seemed to be in an ecstasy of praise; and nor was she alone. Many of the other men and women seemed to be in the grip of emotions deeper than I could fathom or begin to understand.

And so we set sail

Chapter 9
A perilous voyage

The sixth day of the voyage found me lying on my hammock feeling barely alive after three days of sickness that had seemed likely to wrench my insides from their moorings. All around me I could hear the sounds of suffering - moans, sighs, sobs and prayers: 'Lord have mercy, Lord have mercy,' or, simply. 'Jesus, Jesus, Jesus.' For three days I had been unable to partake of a single morsel of food, and imagined I could feel my flesh melting from my bones. However, on that sixth morning, weak though I was, I felt distinctly improved in health; and my appearance must have reassured Mammy, for she forced me to sit up, wrapped my blanket around my shoulders and draped a shawl over my head.

'We goin' on deck,' she announced. 'Fresh air de only medicine you need now.'

I sank back with a groan. 'Mammy, my foot too weak. They not goin' be able to carry me up.'

She wasted no time trying to persuade me otherwise — simply put her strong arm around me and forced me to stand. For a moment I thought I would vomit again. My head swam, the cabin went black, and a clammy sweat broke out all over my body; but I could feel Mammy's arm supporting me and hear her encouraging words. In a short while my head cleared and we were able to proceed, though very slowly, to the deck. As usual, Mammy was proved right, for after I had recovered from the first shock of the freezing cold, I found myself breathing in the pure tangy air in great gulps as if it were spring water and I had been dying of thirst. After some moments I was able to tell her that I was feeling much better.

'What I done tell you?' she said with satisfaction. 'From today, me an' you goin' be up here every mornin' befo' we pray, an' every evenin' after we done eat. De place stinkin' to de sky down dere an' we takin' in de same bad breeze over an' over again... Dat why you been so sick.'

'But why you not sick, Mammy?' I asked. 'You done take in de same bad breeze like everybody else.'

Mammy chuckled in her special way. 'Chile,' she said, 'you Mammy like a ol' oak tree. If dey don' take a axe to me, notin' goin' bring me down.' 'Oh, Mammy!' I said, weakly joining her laughter.

'Is true,' she insisted.

Prayers were held in the one large room where we also met for meals. Every morning we were reminded of Mr. Clarkson's advice to us and as a result, life on board was as tranquil as it was possible for it to be with the number of children in our midst. I doubted that the passengers on board the other transports gave as much heed to Mr. Clarkson's admonitions as we did. Everyone on the *Lucretia* was conscious of his presence on board even though he was confined to his cabin by his indisposition.

My mother succeeded in converting several of our fellow passengers to her enthusiasm for fresh air and as the days passed, most people found their sea legs. I myself had completely recovered and was in great demand as a childminder. We were thus settling down satisfactorily when disaster struck.

For the whole of the day on which it occurred, I had observed that the sky was coloured a peculiar leaden grey, and that the habitual rolling and heaving of the ship and the creaking of her aged timbers were increasing. Towards evening we went on deck for our usual constitutional and were still there when the force of the wind suddenly strengthened; we had to hasten below or risk being blown overboard. Then, confined below decks, and ignorant of what was happening above us, our fears multiplied, for we could hear sounds of frenzied activity and shouted instructions in between the noise of crashing objects, terrified shrieks and wailing. Within minutes our happy ship became a floating hell. My hammock swung wildly to and fro with the violent movements; my arms ached with the effort it took to cling to it. In a little while, retching and vomiting, moans and prayers started again.

'Oh...Oh,...Oh,'moaned Sister Bella Appleby, a woman from Shelburne who was one of the people sharing our cabin. 'Who been force me to leave Scotia? Is true life been hard, but we was livin' ... Now we all goin' die.'

'Hush, Bella,' Mammy said as Mrs. Appleby broke into a loud wailing. . 'Who done tol' you we all goin' die? You tink de Lord done bring we all dis way jus' for we to die befo' we even see Afnca? Where you faith?'

In a loud firm voice, Mammy began to recite the psalm with which we had so confidently started our journey. 'God is our refuge and strength, a very present help in trouble ...' I tried to join in, but words which I had known by heart since the age of nine had flown clear out of my head, whereas, only the tossing of the ship made Mammy's voice falter. Throughout those dreadful hours, she recited one psalm after another, then sang hymns and prayed aloud. Everyone drew strength and comfort from her calmness and fortitude.

By the next morning the wind had dropped. The decks remained drenched and slippery from the torrents of water which had poured over them, but only lowering clouds and the continuing roughness of the sea gave evidence of the night just passed. People's faces showed that they had survived an ordeal, and we were a subdued assembly that morning - more subdued because not one of the other vessels was in sight; we feared that they had perished beneath the waves.

Our faith was further tried in the following days, for hard on the heels of the gale came an outbreak of the bloody flux and shaking fevers. Only the open decks were free of the nauseating stench that now seemed to fill every nook and cranny of the ship so that, in spite of the weather which remained blustery and exceedingly cold, those of us who had hitherto escaped the pestilence increased the time we spent outside. Mammy's assurance to Mrs. Appleby proved to be false, for people began to die. It seemed that every other day we were assembled on deck to commit to a watery grave another body wrapped in a canvas shroud. I shuddered the first time I heard the heavy splash as the body hit the water, but I learned something on that voyage: that it is possible to become hardened to experiences one would have thought unbearable in normal times. In all, ten people died on the *Lucretia*. Sadly, Sister Bella realised her worst fears; she passed away after three days of suffering. Old Auntie Joanna who had been ill before we left Nova Scotia also died, as did Mr. Rose, Mr. Petrie, Mrs. Wilkie and her little daughter, Anne; all went within a few days of each other.

An air of gloom and despondency hung over the *Lucretia,* but we continued to make steady progress southwards and, as the days went by, our drooping spirits were by degrees forced upward with the marked improvement in the weather. The clear blue of cloudless skies, caressing breezes, and the now gentle roll of the waves, all restored cheer to our hearts. The sickness continued, but as more people became well enough to sit out on the deck, its virulence abated. I needed no persuasion to spend as much time as possible there now that I could remove my shawl and stockings and bask in the sunshine. It was such bliss to feel the touch of a light breeze on my bare skin that I envied my little charges who were allowed to run about in the skimpiest of clothing.

Farther and farther south we sailed; the breezes grew warmer, and the gentle movement of the ship reminded me of a leaf floating down a river on a summer afternoon. Even those who had been most racked by sickness could at last emerge from below. The month of February drew to a close and the voyage itself reached a peak of tediousness. I had grown tired of the lack of variety in our diet, and of having to mingle with the same small group of people day after day. Above all, it was the sea itself that wearied my spirit. Day after day, its grey - green expanse, sometimes dull, sometimes shimmering, stretched as far as the eye could see - endless emptiness except for the birds that occasionally perched on the deck - rails, or the flying fish which suddenly appeared, glittered for a moment above the water before disappearing as if they had been phantoms. We still had not sighted the other transports.

Then came the month of March. Birds appeared more frequently, and in greater numbers, wheeling about the masts, uttering sharp, shrill cries. It was towards the end of the first week, on what was to be our fiftieth day at sea, that we were awakened by cries of, 'Land ahoy! 'Land ahoy!' just as the dawn was breaking. Tidying ourselves with all speed, we rushed to the top deck where a welcome sight greeted our eyes. Several ships lay peacefully at anchor; we rightly took them to be some of the transports we had feared never to see again. They must have made swifter progress before the wind and arrived some days earlier. Shouts of joy disturbed the quiet of the morning; our own ship's anchor hit the water with a great splash.

The land was only faintly outlined in the pale dawn light and, at first; all were too occupied with expressions of joy and gratitude, and in the giving and receiving of jubilant embraces to pay it much attention. Mr. Clarkson's admonitions were all but forgotten in the excitement. In fact, the scene on deck had become quite disorderly when that gentleman himself arrived there. Quiet was restored, in part out of respect for his authority, but also, on account of his appearance of extreme ill health. People shook their heads and muttered sadly over the way his clothes hung on his shrunken frame. It was in a hoarse voice that he said,

'My friends, here we are arrived safely on the shores of Sierra Leone. We have experienced danger and discomfort, but the good Lord has seen fit to deliver us.'

'Hallelujah!'

'Let me thank you all,' he went on after that fervent response, 'for observing my rules of conduct so faithfully that I have received no complaints except of sickness. There is much hard work ahead of us, but you have proved your mettle; I have no doubt that we can overcome any difficulties that may await us here...I now call upon Captain George to lead the thanksgiving.'

Tears drenched Pastor George's cheeks as, in ringing tones, he said, 'I love the Lord because he hath heard my voice and my supplications. Because he hath inclined his ear unto me, therefore will I call upon him as long as I live. The sorrows of death compassed me and the pains of hell gat hold upon me. I found trouble and sorrow. Then I called upon the name of the Lord. O Lord, I beseech thee to deliver my soul. Gracious is the Lord and righteous. Yea, our God is merciful!'

More shouts of 'Hallelujah!' and 'Hosanna' echoed around the deck as the sun began to climb in the sky. Up and up it came, pouring light over the anchored ships and the still dark water. By that same light we had our first look at our new country.

It appeared that we had sailed up a river for, on our left, at some distance from the ships, we could see a low- lying, wooded shore. On our right we gazed, as if spellbound, at an enchanting landscape of mountains, dark with forests - mountains which seemed to rise from the sea itself. The pale sky above them was tinted with delicate shades of pink, red, grey, magenta and purple which gradually became shot with a burning orange light. My heart contracted with a sudden pang, perhaps of joy, though any happiness I felt was not so much for myself as for Bro and, above all, for Mammy. On that first glorious morning, it was possible to believe that we had indeed reached the Promised Land.

PART TWO

Chapter 10
Freetown

Two boats had been lowered from the *Lucretia*, and Mr. Clarkson, with a party of men, including Bro and Pastor George, set out for a closer inspection of the land. Those of us who remained aboard busied ourselves collecting our belongings for, having been told that there were already Company officials ashore, we assumed we would be able to disembark that very day. It was not to be; not that day, nor for several days to come.

The men returned late in the afternoon, and it was immediately clear that some bitter disappointment had met the shore party. Knots of people grumbled together on the deck, some making angry gestures, while others listened with scowls. When we sought to discover the cause of their anger, at first Bro merely shook his head and muttered something about lazy fools thinking about nothing but their own importance and how well turned out they were in their uniforms. So great was his vexation that several minutes passed before he answered Mammy's anxiously repeated, 'What happen, Bro? ... What happen over yonder?'

Finally, he took a deep breath and said, 'Mammy, we goin' pass a hard time again, I kin tell you. Is not Mr. Clarkson fault ... He, heself, so boilin' wit' rage I kin wager anytin', dis minute he writin' to London to tell dem what done happen.'

'But what happen, Bro?' Mammy asked again, this time with some impatience.

Bro then told us that when the shore party landed, they were met by seven Company officials strutting like kings, in cockaded hats, epauletted coats, and swords slapping their breeches.

'Dey say dey de canc'llors,' he said, and spat on the deck. 'Some of dem stinkin' wit' rum yet dey tryin' to look like dey jus' finish to make de worl'. Dey tell Mr. Clarkson dat he not de only one wit' autority over we;... dat de Company say he got to rule together wit' dem...An' all de time dey lookin' at we like we some low creature ... When I tink how we done lef' Scotia to run away from people like dat - den here dey is again to torment we ... I tell you, Mammy, right now I fit squeeze somebody troat ... An' den when Mr. Clarkson ask why only two small piece of groun' done clear for we an' no shelter ready, dey answer him dat day don' see why de Company got to pay for labour when we kin clear de lan' for weself. Mr. Clarkson dumb wit' rage. He face turnin' red an' white by turn, an' he shakin' from head to foot.'

'An' de poor man not even strong yet,' Mammy said.

But she took the disturbing news quite calmly; only asked whether the land itself looked promising, at which question Bro's stormy countenance brightened.

'Oh, yes, de lan' look fine, Mammy. Tomorrow we goin' start clearin' to make a road. When we done finish you all goin' be able to go ashore an' see for youself. Plenty good timber tree, plenty tree wit' fruit, fresh water stream nearby... An' when we crossin' over I see plenty fine-lookin' fish swimmin' aroun'. When you reach, you got to climb some, den de groun' a bit flat, den you meet one high hill dey callin' St George's Hill. '

'Bro,' Mammy interrupted, 'if we got to work, we goin' work. We done use hard work so notin' too bad done happen yet.'

'Maybe you right,' Bro said, somewhat appeased. 'Oh, I done forget' to tell you; we hear tell all in all sixty- five people dead from de flux an' fever.'

'Ah well,' Mammy said, 'all dey own trouble done finish now. Is we lef' to carry on de battle.'

By this time there was so much noise on the deck that Pastor George had to remind us that Mr. Clarkson's rules were still to be observed. He also delivered a message from Mr. Clarkson that women and children would remain in the transports for the time being, but all able-bodied men should report for land clearing the following day.

Eager to renew my acquaintance with Felicia Porter I was keenly disappointed, but what cannot be cured must be endured; like everyone else, I had to contain my impatience to the best of my ability.

Land clearing began in earnest the following morning, and for several days we saw nothing of our menfolk; they lived ashore in temporary shelters. However, we could see the progress being made as day by day more red earth became visible. Our days were enlivened by the arrival of small boats carrying native men and boys, hoping to trade with us. They did not look like the savages of my imagination, though the boys were as naked as the day they were born and displayed in a most shocking fashion, those parts of the body modesty demands should be covered. The men rowed from ship to ship, grinning in a friendly way as they held aloft bunches of strange fruits and vegetables. Only the sailors offered to buy any of their wares. The boys dived from their shallow craft and stayed below the surface of the water while we held our breaths in fear for their lives. Just when we thought they had surely perished, they reappeared like dark porpoises, their mouths stretched from ear to ear in happy, gleaming grins. One of the sailors threw a coin into the water; they dived again and in a matter of seconds had retrieved the coin from the depths below. I never tired of watching them perform that feat and looked forward to their daily appearance.

Not until the following Sunday, the eleventh day of March, were we allowed to set foot on the shore. Sailors rowed us across the river, and we had to climb a flight of crude steps cut into the high incline, before reaching the more gently sloping ground Bro had described. The scene that met our eyes was one of colourful confusion. For the first time, I saw natives unattached to boats - middle-aged men in rough homespun garments, a few of a lighter complexion with higher noses and thinner lips. The latter were dressed either in long gowns resembling nightshirts, or in tunics worn over drawers that billowed about their calves like limp sails. All of them wore close fitting cloth caps. Other men and boys, barefooted for the most part, had on tattered shirts and breeches. Naked children darted in and out of the motley throng, while flat-chested girls of about my age or younger, stood gazing wide-eyed at these people who were as dark-skinned as they were, yet so different in all other respects. These maidens were naked except for a narrow apron that hung from their waists and down the length of their thighs in front and behind. Many were the disapproving remarks about their skimpy apparel, but the sight of the grown women was what made our matrons purse their lips with expressions of disgust.

The reason for this behaviour was that those native women not carrying babies strapped to their backs with cloths up to their armpits, were from their waists up as naked as God made them. No, that is not entirely accurate; they wore earrings, and their necks were adorned with necklaces of glass beads or some other material. There they stood, gracefully erect, and quite unashamed as they looked us over. Perhaps I should have been more disturbed by their exposed breasts, but after my first shocked glance, I quickly became more interested in the hair arrangements revealed by those with uncovered heads; never before had I seen hair woven neatly on the scalp like a kind of embroidery. For a while I quite forgot my original intention of seeking out Felicia Porter at the earliest opportunity. When I did remember, it took a determined search to spot her in the crowd.

Overjoyed to find each other safe and well, we embraced; stood back to laugh into each other's eyes then embraced again, eager questions spilling from our lips. Out of the corner of my eye I saw a young man watching this scene of delighted reunion with amusement.

'What you smilin' at, you Junius?' Felicia said in pretended indignation when she noticed his expression. 'Dis my frien' Deannie Dixon. You 'member I been tell you 'bout dem people I meet in Halifax?'

'Ah, so dis de Deannie Dixon ...' the young man said, drawing closer.

I was grateful to have a dark complexion that day, for my cheeks grew warm at the look of admiration Junius Porter gave me. I dropped my eyes quickly and, observing my discomfort, Felicia gave him a playful shove.

'Don' pay my broda no mine, Deannie; he jus' love to jest. Never serious.'

At which, pretending vexation, Junius Porter remarked that good sisters did not speak ill of their brothers. Before Felicia could make a suitable retort a bell rang out, summoning us to assemble; we would come to know it well.

We moved with the crowd towards a massive tree, which I now know to be the silk-cotton tree. On its broad branches squatted some wide-eyed, furry creatures whose long, thick tails hung straight down behind them like ropes. There was something strangely human about the way they sat there, gibbering as they watched the activity below. Every few minutes one of them would break away from the group and swing from one branch to the next, using its tail as a fifth limb.

A wooden platform had been erected in the shade provided by the giant tree; on it stood Mr. Clarkson, the leaders of our various congregations, a man in a surplice, and the seven Councillors of whom we had received such unfavourable reports. Most of the Councillors seemed to be sniffing as if we smelt bad — which was quite likely, I must admit, after so many weeks spent cooped up aboard the transports. I noticed other pale faces, both male and female, among the people standing closest to the platform and took them to be various Company employees and their womenfolk.

Mr. Clarkson eventually held up his hand for silence and the man in a surplice stepped forward (I later learned that he was Mr. Nathaniel Gilbert, Chaplain of the Sierra Leone Company). After Pastor George's resonant utterances, his voice was a disappointment - reedy and weak, which I thought unworthy of such a momentous occasion. He read out a prayer, preached on the text, 'Unless the Lord build a house, they labour in vain that build it,' read out another prayer, then announced a familiar hymn.

'Wake every heart and every tongue
To praise the Saviour's name.
The day of Jubilee is come
Return ye ransomed sinners home.'

Our voices might have been heard in the mansions of heaven as we sang that Sunday morning. We certainly disturbed the wide-eyed creatures who, for the rest of the proceedings, never stopped leaping from branch to branch. The man in the surplice pronounced the Benediction, then gave way to Mr. Clarkson who, despite being in full military attire himself, looked as pale and exhausted as ever. In as strong a voice as he could muster, he made an announcement that brought a long, loud cheer:

'According to the wishes of the Directors of the Sierra Leone Company, I declare this place to be named from henceforth, Free Town. Long may it prosper!' We dispersed soon afterwards and, though sorry to be parted from Felicia again, it was in a jolly mood that I returned with the others to our floating quarters.

CHAPTER 11
Settlers unsettled

Another week passed before sufficient ground had been cleared to allow the rest of us to leave the ships for good. By that time the soaring temperatures and our confinement on board had made life almost unbearable. If we stayed in our cramped and airless quarters below decks, the fetid air seemed likely to stifle us, but if we stayed too long on the open deck before the late afternoon, sunlight shimmering on the water strained our eyes to the point of tears. Every day, even before the morning was far advanced, rivulets of water ran down my body, making my garments cling to my skin in a most unpleasant way. And the nights were worse than the daylight hours; all we could do was toss and turn, vainly attempting to sleep.

I remember overhearing two women discussing the heat as they fanned themselves with their hats. One said,

'We been say Scotia too col'; ... we gettin' all de heat we want now, eh?'

To which the other replied,

'You said it, sister. Bring to mine Car'lina in high summer.   If it goin' be like dis all de time, we soon goin' be black as pitch or else melted clean away wit' all dis sweatin' ... Whew!'

I leave the reader to imagine our delight at being freed from that hellish place. However, I soon discovered that life ashore was not without tribulations of its own.

On my previous visit to Freetown, I had been fully occupied with my first sight of the native women, my reunion with Felicia and the exhilaration of the moment. Now that we were to be permanently ashore, I took a good look around me, and what I saw filled me with a peculiar dread. In those early days, our 'town' was no more than a vast clearing that would have been entirely surrounded by thick forest, had it not been for the ocean to the north, east, and west, and the few paths leading out of it. The huge trees and curling vines seemed almost alive, and somehow threatening - as if they were preparing to crowd these usurpers into the sea. So overwhelmed did I feel at first that, apart from the massive tree under whose branches our settlement had been named, the only other trees that made an impression on me were coconut palms - so very slender, yet soaring skywards without any support that I could see. How, I asked myself, could a tree be so slender, yet grow to such a height? It was another of nature's mysteries that so often filled me with wonder.

Our accommodation was in makeshift shelters such as had already been erected for the men - stout wooden posts driven into the ground and covered in sail cloth. Now that I was older, I found it hard to fall asleep on the rough ground with only a couple of blankets to protect me; and all night long a host of mosquitoes and unknown insects stung and bit any uncovered skin. The eerie calls of nocturnal creatures added to my uneasiness, as did the sound of drumming that came from the direction of the native village to the west. I imagined all manner of sinister rituals and moved as close to Mammy as possible. When I eventually fell asleep, it was with my head pressed against her broad back.

Towards the end of our second week ashore, in the middle of the night, there came a shout of, 'Snake, snake!' from the other end of our shelter - such a shriek it was that we scrambled up in panic and shook out our coverings amid much shouting and heavy thuds. Rudely awakened, the infants bawled and refused to be hushed.

I had no recollection of ever seeing a snake, though Bro and Mammy had spoken of them. When, by the flickering light of a lantern, I saw the thick, dark, slithery coils of the vile creature as it lay dead, I felt that I would never be able to sleep again until our dwelling had proper doors and windows. Fortunately for my peace of mind, some streets had begun to be laid out, which meant that building plots would soon be distributed.

Meanwhile, the general state of affairs in Freetown, as we had already begun to call our new home, was causing anxiety and discontent. Having deceived themselves that titles and external trappings made them men of stature and consequence, the Councillors daily used their position to bully and insult our menfolk. Many times I heard Bro growl, 'If not for Mr. Clarkson!'

Like the other men, the greatest part of his anger stemmed from the fact that he had not expected to be still under the yoke of white masters, especially men who, with the exception of Mr. Clarkson and another Councillor called Mr. Dawes, he considered unworthy of respect. The Councillors' bad manners might have been excused had they been competent overseers; according to Bro, at the time part of the team erecting company buildings, it was as if they had been employed not to build the settlement but to thwart all efforts in that direction. He complained that one Councillor would issue an order only for another to change it without reason. Poor Mr. Clarkson, now being addressed as 'Govnor', was supposed to be in charge of the Councillors but he seemed to have little control over them.

To give just one example of this sorry state of affairs, not long after we arrived, Dr. Bell, the Company doctor, dropped dead. Since his sudden demise was rumoured to be the result of his addiction to rum, the reader will easily imagine the derisive mutterings among our people when they learnt that he would be buried with pomp and ceremony.

Indeed, resplendent in their best uniforms, and led by a fifer and drummer, Mr. Clarkson and his Councillors marched behind the coffin in a solemn procession. As was expected, we fell in behind them with due respect. Only after the funeral did we learn, by the old Birchtown method, that Mr. Clarkson had wished for the simplest of Christian burials for Dr. Bell's drink-sodden corpse, but had been overruled by the Councillors who argued that a hasty burial would diminish a white man in the eyes of Negroes. They even ordered a gun salute for Dr. Bell, thus causing a real tragedy. Through some miscalculation, the poor young gunner lost an arm and subsequently his life.

We did not know the reason for his stiff demeanour at the time, but it was with his jaw noticeably clenched that Mr. Clarkson led the solemn procession. Just before we reached the burial ground, he staggered and almost fell; we feared the worst, but he had only swooned, no doubt overcome by heat and anger.

Each day, at half past the hour of five in the morning, cannon boomed to awaken us. One hour later, except on Sundays, the bell rang out, summoning the men to work. They laboured until eight o'clock, were then allowed a free hour to partake of their breakfast, after which they continued to work until eleven o'clock. All labour ceased for three hours during the hottest part of the day, but when it resumed, continued until the firing of the cannon at sunset.

The reader should bear in mind that our men were not accustomed to working in conditions of such oppressive heat. Besides, their hands were now covered with painful calluses, and their lower legs cut about by the sharp edges of a type of grass that grew in profusion everywhere. To make matters worse, they were always hungry. We were all hungry, for even before the end of March the provisions brought from Nova Scotia had begun to be rationed. Each day we scanned the horizon, hoping to spot the supply ship we so eagerly awaited. One did arrive, but to our utter disappointment, carried only a large consignment of watering cans. We looked for another in vain.

In the first week of April, Mr. Clarkson informed the heads of families that until further notice, everyone in Freetown would have to go on half rations when full rations had been barely sufficient to maintain Mammy and me in strength, not to mention our menfolk who did more than seven hours of hard labour every single day, except Sunday. As fear gripped our hearts, the men's simmering resentment came to a boil.

Chapter 12
The fall of Thomas Peters

The Company officials still used ships in the harbour as sleeping quarters. When they left the settlement that evening, word went round that heads of families and their dependants should meet under the silk cotton tree. The meeting concluded that a spokesman was needed to deal with Mr. Clarkson and the Council on our behalf.

From the first, Thomas Peters had been one of the loudest in his condemnation of the Council. After the role he had played in bringing us to Sierra Leone, it came as no surprise that he was elected spokesman and given the grand title of 'Speaker General.' He immediately requested all heads of families to sign a petition protesting the lack of food, proper shelter, and the fact that, so far, no move had been made to survey the promised acres of farmland.

Pastor George spoke out against this proposal at once, saying that whether we liked it or not, Mr. Clarkson and the Council had been put in authority over us by the Sierra Leone Company, which had brought us to Africa. He said it was our Christian duty not to rebel against the Council but instead to show our gratitude by being still before the Lord and waiting patiently for him. 'We done wait so long,' he declared in his powerful voice. 'We kin wait lil bit more.'

Members of our Baptist congregation listened to him in respectful silence even though, from the shaken heads and mutterings, it was plain to see that not many shared his opinion. Not so the Methodists. Old Pastor Wilkinson shouted, 'You never hear tell dat de Lord help people who tryin' to help deyself?'

'You fit to die talkin' for dem whitefolk,' was another, more shocking cry. 'You done forget already what happen las' time we wait?'

Despite more abuse from the Methodists, Pastor George stood firm.

'You kin do what you want, but I not goin' support dis action; an' I pray none of my own people goin' follow dis road of foolishness.'

In the end, only one hundred and thirty-two people signed the petition - all of them Methodists except for a handful of Huntingdonians. Not a single Baptist signed it, and from that day began a hostility between Baptists and Methodists that lasted many a year.

What happened after we had dispersed is forever shrouded in mystery; the Methodists believed Pastor George had a hand in it, but that was stoutly denied and never proved. The next morning, which was Easter Sunday, the bell summoned us to assemble long before the normal hour for a worship service. As usual, we gathered under the silk cotton tree. On the platform stood Mr. Clarkson, his Councillors and the Chaplain. Mr. Clarkson looked more haggard than ever, with shadows like dark bruises under his sunken eyes.

He gazed at us somewhat sadly for several moments before beginning to speak in a voice of quiet intensity.

'So... As if we do not have enough troubles, we now have a traitor in our midst.' He paused to let that startling information sink in before going on. 'Do you know the lawful punishment for traitors? Were it not for the love of God in my heart, this day one should swing from this very tree... Thomas Peters, I ask you to come forward.'

An audible gasp rose from our ranks. I tiptoed and stretched my neck to catch a glimpse of Thomas Peters, but everyone else was likewise engaged. Not until he had climbed onto the platform himself was it possible to see him. Mr. Clarkson now addressed him face to face.

'So you seek to make yourself the Governor of this place...'

Thomas Peters's jaw dropped; shaking his head from side to side, he seemed about to speak, but Mr. Clarkson gave him no time to utter a word.

'You are a disappointment to me, man,' he went on. 'When first we met, I hoped to have an able helper in my chosen task, but it now appears that you are trying to undermine my authority.' Turning back to us, he spoke with unusual sternness,

'And as for the rest of you... Let me remind you that but for the sacrifices made by the men of goodwill who own the Sierra Leone Company, you would still be shivering in the snows of Nova Scotia. Even if you have no loyalty to the Company I had hoped for loyalty to me after the devotion I have shown to your cause. You can see that my health is uncertain; only my concern for your welfare has made me stay here this long ... and... and this treachery is the gratitude I receive?'

His voice faltered and dropped as he said those words; I saw two of the Councillors exchange malicious smirks. Presently, Mr. Clarkson continued in a firmer tone.

'Evidently, you think Thomas Peters would have made of Freetown a paradise by now were he the Governor. You may have him if you so desire; but make your choice now or forever hold your peace.' There was much shuffling and muttering, but not one person moved or spoke in support of Thomas Peters. He decided it was time to speak up for himself and did so in a strong and almost scornful voice.

'Dey done tell you lie, Sir, who ever gone runnin' to you in de night. My people only choose me to talk for dem befo' you an' de Can'cil. We tinkin' de Can'cil fit to know how we feel 'bout what happenin' here - dat's all. Nobody tryin' to be Gov'nor over you head.'

In the ensuing silence, Mr. Clarkson looked deep into Thomas Peters's eyes as if to learn therein whether or not to believe him. He must have been satisfied with what he saw, for when he spoke again, it was in a milder manner.

'I am fully aware that all is not well here, but I beseech you; trust me and exercise patience. All new ventures are fraught with difficulties. You say you have no land; you will receive your land - all the acres promised to you. I give you my word of honour. Any day now, the other supply ship will arrive and the present shortage of food will cease. Meanwhile, let us help one another like Christians...I beseech you.'

The Chaplain took his place, and we proceeded with the worship service for Easter Sunday; but our hearts were not in it; our singing was subdued.

To the relief of all, the supply ship eventually arrived, but apart from more adequate provisions, our general situation remained the same. Disapproval of the Council continued unabated, Thomas Peters among the most outspoken critics. I shall be running ahead of the sequence of events, but I think it appropriate to complete his part in this story now, for he lived but two months more.

A few weeks after his public confrontation with Mr. Clarkson came public humiliation. One of the settlers from Annapolis, a man called Cato Goldsmith, died of the sickness which began on the voyage to Sierra Leone and had remained with us. Freetown reeled from shock when the rumour went around that his widow had complained to Mr. Clarkson that Thomas Peters entered her house by force, ransacked her late husband's belongings and stole money. This time the rumour seemed well founded for Mr. Clarkson had Thomas Peters arrested, charged him with theft and misconduct, then ordered a trial by jury.

It was a painful affair. Thomas Peters did not deny that he had taken the money but he refused to admit that he stole it. He told the jury that Cato Goldsmith owed him the amount he took, that his widow had refused to pay the debt and that he had only seized what was rightfully his. Since the widow could not convince the jury that his allegations were false, Thomas Peters was acquitted of that charge. However, the jury found him guilty of misconduct as charged. Mr. Clarkson censured him in public and ordered him to return every penny. After that, Thomas Peters became a changed man. Gone was the proud bearing of the respected Speaker General. His shoulders slumped, and his face lost all animation. Late in June he, too, fell ill with the dreaded flux and in a matter of days was dead and buried.

Among our Baptist congregation some expressed the view that his downfall and early death were a judgement from heaven against one who had behaved ungratefully. Mammy had her own opinion of the matter.

'Is a bitter heart,' she said. 'Notin' goin' put a person in Satan han' like a bitter heart. Thomas

Peters been disappoint, an' I not blamin' him for dat. Is because he been bol' an' brave dat we sittin' here today. Gov'nor Clarkson been fit to give him a important position here; make him canc'llor even.'

'Canc'llor?' Bro said with raised eyebrows, 'but Mammy, is not Gov'nor who make de canc'llor, else we not get dem ninnynonny here, struttin' round confusin' de place.

'Maybe not canc'llor,' Mammy conceded, 'but sometin' important. De man been have plenty good sense in he head; ...an' he brave. I sorry he been bitter so.'

Chapter 13
A tragedy befalls the Dixon family

By the middle of May, eight of Freetown's streets had been laid out in the form of a gridiron - five going straight up the hill in a southerly direction from the northern side of the waterfront, and three others traversing them from east to west; eventually, there would be nine streets going from north to south. Around this time, Bro received his building lot. It was on the corner formed by the intersection of the fourth street from the east and the topmost traversing street; that location provided a sweeping view of the ocean.

Bro and Daniel erected a frame of sticks and fashioned a roof out of long grasses. Mammy and I sought and found a clay bed from which we filled in the gaps in the walls and plastered them over; we cleared the earth within the walls of vegetation and loose gravel, and trampled it to a semblance of smoothness. Our first home in Freetown was hardly larger than our cabin in Birchtown, but it had a door, and windows which could be shut tight - for me the most important consideration. We entered the house by way of a porch just wide enough to accommodate two chairs placed side by side. In the late afternoons Mammy and I would sit in this little nook to catch the breeze while we waited for Bro and Daniel to return from their work.

We were thus installed in our usual place at the usual time, a few days after Thomas Peters's funeral. Since I had already acquired something of a reputation as a needle - woman, on my lap lay a frock I was making up for the wife of one of the Company officials; Mammy was helping me put the finishing touches to another. It had rained for a short while a few hours earlier and the sky remained a dense mass of water - laden clouds. Moisture rose like steam from the ground and muggy air pressed in on us from every side. Speaking required such an effort that our conversation had died away.

We were still working in silence when Mammy heaved a deep sigh and for some moments stared moodily towards the ocean, her hands lying idle on her lap. Not once since our arrival in Sierra Leone had I heard Mammy sigh in just that way - not once in all the difficult days we had endured. Instead, she had remained steadfastly cheerful and, as always, did her best to sustain our spirits. It was therefore in some alarm that I enquired what ailed her. She turned towards me, seemed to hesitate, then said, '

'Deannie, I been wantin' to talk to you for long. De time done come.'

Something in her tone of voice made my heart skip a beat; with growing alarm I asked again, 'Mammy, you feelin' bad?'

'No. chile,' she said returning to the frock on her lap, 'I not feelin' bad, but las' night I done dream again ... In de dream I seen you an' Dan and Bro, sittin' in de house wit' plenty people comin an' goin', comin' an' goin'. You all wearin' Sunday clothes. I seen Pastor George, an' Broda Isaacs. I seen Sister Sophia from across de street, an' Licia an' her broda... many people. But you know sometin'? I myself not in de dream; is like I only watchin' you all from afar. I tinkin' 'bout dat dream jus' now an' wonderin' what it mean; wonderin' if perhaps de Lord gettin' ready to call me home. ..'

My heart leapt. What was Mammy talking about? That she might soon be dead? The very thought of such a calamity
made me cry out,

'Mammy, don' talk so!'

'If I talk or I don' talk, whatever got to be goin' be,' Mammy answered.

'But...but you always sayin' you strong.'

'So I say, Deannie, an' is true; but when de Lord ready for you, it don' matter how you feelin'; ... You got to be ready to go.'

Mammy sounded so resigned, that tears filled my eyes and overflowed, rolling down my cheeks. Work forgotten, I fell on my knees and buried my face in her lap, wracked with pain. She allowed me to weep for some moments, gently stroking the back of my neck; then said again, 'De time done come for me to talk to you.'

I shook my head against her skirts, but she took me by the chin and forced me to look at her; her own cheeks were as wet as mine. 'Get up an' sit down, chile. If de Lord goin' call me home, I got to do my duty befo' I go.'

I shook my head more violently and she al-lowed me to remain where I was.

'You 'member I been tell you how Bro' an' me not been wed befo' I born Daniel an' you, but we been wed when we reach Scotia? Well, many of we people still not wed, not even now. Dey goin' to church every day but dey still carryin' on wit'out de blessin' of de Lord - carryin' on an' breedin' children an' all. Dey don' tink what dey doin' is wrong, but I tink is wrong. You know why? Because dey behavin' like dey still slave. People who free fit be wed good an' proper, like decent whitefolk ... Reason I tellin' you dis is because I knows men. Even de one who got day own woman in de house, soon as dey see one fine looking girl, dey ready to come sniffin' roun' sweet-talkin' her. Nex' tin' she know, she carryin' a baby under her skirt...You almost a woman now, Deannie, and you a fine girl - such a fine girl,' she added, stroking the back of my head again. 'Maybe I not goin' be here to look out for you...' She gave me a look so full of sad tenderness that my tears welled up anew.

'Jus' now dey goin' come sniffin' roun', an' if I under de groun' I not goin' lie easy if I know you behavin' like a slave. We free people now, so

I want you to promise me on you baptism, you never goin' carry on wit' no man till you done wed ... I don' want my girl havin' no child wit' no man who not her lawful wedded husband. You children goin' be free born. Dey fit be born in a proper fam'ly, you hear me?'

Such was the turmoil in my heart and mind that I could only stare at her like a dumb creature, hardly understanding what she was talking about. Certainly, having lived in a community like ours, where every family kept chickens or hogs, and dogs roamed freely, I had often observed the male and female animals engage in a peculiar coupling; but I had looked on it as animal behaviour and never connected their antics with producing their young. Neither had I ever wondered how, as was commonly the case, women gave birth to children without having husbands that I knew of. Mammy had never encouraged my childish questions about the origin of babies, saying only, 'Plenty time to know 'bout all dat when you bigger.' When I did achieve a certain maturity, she said, 'Now you big enough to born you own chile', but still did not enlighten me as to how this miracle would occur. Having come to the conclusion that in God's good time I also would become a mother, I had felt no need to press her for further explanations. To my benumbed mind, she now seemed to be telling me that the begetting of children was the result of some manner of contact between a man and a woman. Why else would she have come to her demand for my promise by first speaking about the ways of men? Oh, but what a time to make such a revelation and in so vague a manner! Tears rained down my cheeks in a fresh torrent, for I realised that had Mammy not been thinking that she might soon leave this earth, she would have continued to keep me in ignorance while making sure there was no opportunity for 'carryin' on' before I left my father's house for a husband's. But what did she mean by 'carryin' on'? I could only guess.

'Promise me, Deannie,' she urged. 'Promise me.'

Filled with dread, utterly bewildered, weeping all the time, I clung to Mammy's skirts and mumbled a promise. After a while, she said,

'Come on, girl ... Bro an' Danny goin' come back jus' now; go wash you face ...I not goin' say notin ' to dem, so you don' say notin', you hear me?'

Bro remarked on my red and swollen eyes, but Mammy answered easily, 'Oh she been complain 'bout her head hurtin'...I done, give her brimstone an' molasses; she feelin' better now. Not so, Deannie?' Bro gave me an anxious look, for sickness still stalked our little town. My heart felt like a lump of cold wet clay within my chest, but I managed to smile as I assured him that the pain was almost gone.

It was our custom to retire for the night soon after evening prayers. Usually I had no difficulty falling asleep; but that night, between the mosquitoes buzzing greedily about my ears, the suffocating heat, my heavy heart and troubled mind, I found it impossible even to doze. Instead, I lay on my pallet staring, dry - eyed, into the thick darkness. The eerie sounds outside struck my ears like a concert by a choir from hell; the endless and ear piercing chirps of crickets formed the treble chorus, the frogs a raucous bass, while a bat's strident, staccato cry was a solo sung by a fiend. Surely there was another interpretation of Mammy's dream! God would not do that to me - take away my mother when I still needed her. And surely God would not end Mammy's life when it was about to start afresh. Mammy had to be wrong! Yet her dreams had always come true in times past. Why not this time? But we needed her so!

Round and round whirled those nagging thoughts so that it was some time before I became aware that the noise outside had changed to a wild lashing and cracking of branches, and a muffled drumming of rain on the roof. More crashes outside reminded me of the gale we had experienced at sea and I cried out to wake the others. Daniel sat up with a start; Bro and Mammy emerged hurriedly from behind their curtain. Bro straightaway began to pray for our safety but, despite his supplication, our flimsy dwelling proved no protection against nature on the rampage. Even before he said 'Amen', with a horrible tearing sound, our roof was snatched from above our heads all in one piece, as if by a giant hand. Drenched to the skin all at once, for a moment we stood like statues - utterly stunned.

Recovering first, Daniel proposed that we try to reach the Company church. It was an excellent suggestion since the partially completed building, stood fairly close to our street and was one of the sturdiest structures in Freetown. Besides, unlike the store, it was certain to be open. We covered our dripping heads with our soaked blankets, and followed each other into the black night and pouring rain. Daniel led the way. Mammy was the last to leave the house.

It seemed that we had covered no more than twenty yards when a flash of lightning illuminated the scene in a ghastly way. In that same instant I heard a single cry behind me. My first instinct was to run as far and as fast as my feet would carry me, but instead, recognising the voice, I whirled about towards the sound as thunder exploded about my ears. At first, I could see nothing, so black was the night; then another white flash showed me what I would have given my life not to see. Something lay at my feet. I knew at once that it was Mammy's body and that she was dead. Mammy, always so brimful of life, reduced, faster than an eye could blink, to a charred heap of flesh and bone and rags. I shrieked and shrieked like a mad thing and, oblivious of any danger to myself, flung myself upon her. Nothing more do I remember of that dreadful night. When I came to my senses, it was full daylight. I was lying on some sort of bench. Felicia Porter was looking anxiously down at me while behind her were the dazed and drawn faces of Bro, Daniel, Junius Porter, and Sister Sophia Russell, who lived across the street. What were they all doing there? I wondered. And where was I? Where was Mammy? Felicia must have observed the change in my countenance from bewilderment to the agony of knowledge for she knelt down beside me and cradled my head on her chest, murmuring, 'Hush now, hush now,' over and over again. Eventually, I became calm enough to rise and go outside, and saw that there was more to grieve over than Mammy's tragic death. Our promised land was a shambles - a sickening confusion of tufts of roof grass, sail cloth, boxes and sticks, piled higgledy-piggledy, all a sodden mess. Uprooted trees, broken branches and masses of leaves littered the newly cleared ground. It was a scene of chaos and wanton destruction fit to break the stoutest heart. Meanwhile, the rain had ceased, the clouds had rolled away and brilliant sunlight seemed to mock my distress. I retched in painful spasms that brought me to my knees, gasping. We had to bury Mammy that very afternoon as the heat made it impossible for corpses to remain exposed for more than a day. She had been so burned that we could not lay her out with the dignity she deserved, but had to pack her remains into a hastily and roughly constructed coffin like a sack of rubbish. As we prepared her for burial, the pain I felt was a living thing, a rat's teeth clamped tight on some vital part of me. I wept bitterly throughout the short service, but at the graveside my unexpected emotion was rage. Something inside me had become a burning ball of anger and the heat of it dried up my tears. Mammy had left Nova Scotia with such high hopes and such deep faith, yet her last weeks on earth had been full of discomfort and anxiety, only to end in a hideous death. I felt like shaking my fists and howling my rage to the sky. Was God indeed up there that he allowed such an outrage to occur? Was he there when lightning was striking my mother dead? Daniel and Bro stood on either side of me at the graveside and as clods of damp red earth thudded unto Mammy's coffin, Bro began to weep again, lamenting in a broken voice, 'No time to say farewell. Oh, Mammy, no time even to say farewell!' His whole body shook with his sobbing and I, who so often had been comforted by him, now put my arms around him and held him with all my strength. In those moments I felt the last traces of childhood falling away from me like dead skin. Despite all that the preachers had said about the Christian's reward awaiting in heaven, I had firmly believed that righteousness was also rewarded here on earth. Yet my mother, who had been a righteous woman, had been struck down without mercy. What was one to believe? It was not that I lost my belief in God in the days following her death, but that its quality changed. The divine being who had been for me a benevolent guard and guide became not less of a god but rather more of a god - a being too mysterious and distant for little Deannie Dixon to comprehend. I now believed that God was to be feared and worshipped not from the hope of any reward here on earth or even in heaven, but simply because he was God and we, powerless creatures at the mercy of his whims. It was to be many, many months before I could once again call myself a Christian in the sense that, believing the words of Jesus, I could feel love flowing from God towards me.

Mammy's death had another effect on me - one that still fills me with shame; only my desire to be truthful forces me to confess it on these pages. On the day of her burial, I lay on a mat in Sister Sophia's house and, exhausted as I was, refused to give myself over to sleep because I was terrified that Mammy would come and touch me with ghostly fingers.

For weeks after her death, the moment I lay down at night, I clamped my eyelids shut, pulled my head kerchief well down over my ears and forehead and brought my covering up to my chin. In great discomfort from the heat, I stayed that way until it was almost dawn to protect myself against Mammy's ghost – Mammy who, in her lifetime, would have fought even a wild beast to protect me from harm! I realised my foolishness, but only the passage of time rid me of my dread.

Chapter 14
Our first rainy season

The reader will perhaps recall that before we left Nova Scotia, Mr. Clarkson had warned us to expect a wet season in Sierra Leone. I, for one, had anticipated only a longer period of rain such as we had known it in Nova Scotia - heavy, driving rain and squally showers sometimes but, for the most part, gentle rain which would bathe the roof tops and mist the hills. Nothing had prepared me for the rains of Sierra Leone.

Bro and Daniel had replaced our roof in just a few days so we had been able to return to our house before the season began in earnest. Now it was fully upon us and, day after day, the weather forced me to remain cooped up in that hovel while outside it poured as if the clouds had burst open, spilling all the water they contained. Sometimes sheets of rain made a curtain thick enough to conceal the sea and sky. Our hastily reconstructed roof allowed puddles to collect in the hollows of the uneven floor; due to the persistent dampness, grey blotches of mildew stained our dark clothes and gave them a musty smell; Bro had to keep oiling his tools and Daniel his gun to prevent their ruin by rust.

It is unlikely that it rained every hour of every day, but in my memory it was so. In any case, the rainy season deepened our misery for, added to our grief and discomfort, was another shortage of food. There was always a bad - tempered crowd milling around the doors of the

Company store, and if the storekeepers had fallen ill, we returned home empty-handed. Once, days went by without the store being opened; the area around it stank from the rotten and mouldy victuals within. We heard that a king called Naimbana, who ruled in the country north of Freetown, on the other side of the river, had been kind enough to send gifts of food to Mr. Clarkson. As for the rest of us, had we not by this time made the acquaintance of natives from the village to the west, whose ruler was called King Jimmy, and from another to the south, ruled by one Pa Demba, heaven alone knows what would have become of us.

Indeed, the natives who we now knew were called Timmanees, were our salvation. The moment the rain eased a little, there would appear at the door, one of their women or children eager to sell us whatever food they could spare - mangoes, bananas and cassava tubers to which we were unaccustomed at the time. Occasionally, they came with fish, either fresh or smoked; not often, though, because at times rough seas prevented the fishermen from venturing out in their shallow, frail-looking craft.

I made friends with a Timmanee maiden of about ten years of age; Fatu was her name. She was as dark as molasses, slender as a young palm tree, and had the most sparkling eyes and teeth I had ever seen. Ignorant of each other's language, we could not converse, but much was communicated with smiles and gestures. Fish was Fatu's merchandise. She would appear at the door with her wares tied together with palm fronds. I would point to a fish; she would hold up the number of her fingers indicating the price in pennies. I would hold up the number of my own fingers that showed what I was willing to pay. Scowling, she would shake her head and reduce the number of fingers she held up by one. I would shake my head with a fiercer frown and increase the number of fingers I held up by one. Thus we arrived at a price that satisfied us both. Fatu would then remove the fish she had sold me from her bunch, and always, there would be a tiny one which she presented with her widest smile.

During one period in July, hundreds of people fell seriously ill at the same time. Many died. At first, it was possible to weep and grieve as we attended one funeral after another, but as had been my experience during the passage to Africa, we soon grew so accustomed to daily tragedy that as week succeeded week, those of us who had escaped so far would ask with almost idle curiosity, 'How many people been die las' night?' — such was our numbness of feeling.

Bro seemed to sink more and more deeply into the mire of his grief with every passing day. Sometimes he sat for what seemed like hours, clutching his Bible and staring into space. At other times he kept muttering, 'Oh God! Oh God!' till I could have screamed from the strain of it. He aroused my sympathy but, full of sorrow myself, I had no words of consolation to give him; neither did Daniel. Mammy had been our anchor so that, like boats cut adrift, at a time when we should have been closest together, we drifted apart. Since most people in Freetown had their own sorrow to bear, I wonder what would have become of us were it not for Felicia and Junius Porter. They became frequent visitors throughout that dark time, as if Felicia had assigned to herself and Junius the task of restoring cheer to the Dixons' home.

She had found employment as a housemaid with Mrs. Pepys, the wife of the Company's surveyor, and each time she paid us a visit, tried to amuse us with stories, true or exaggerated, of life in the household she served. When Bro rewarded her with a reluctant chuckle once, I could have rewarded her with a kiss. His amusement was caused by her comical description of Mrs. Pepys's encounter with a small lizard in her chest of drawers. How she shrieked and swooned and made Felicia shake out all her clothes and inspect the drawers for the tiniest crack which then had to be sealed with candle wax.

Apart from our own distress and the widespread low spirits, angry mutterings increased among those of our people who believed that once again we were being cheated of our rights. Bad weather prevented Mr. Pepys from surveying and laying out the promised acres, but that did not appease those determined to condemn the Company. Making one of his rare contributions to conversation, Daniel told us that he had heard it said that if the Company intended to give settlers any farm land, the surveying would have been completed before the beginning of the rains.

Only time would tell whether or not that was the truth.

Another bone of contention concerned allocation of building plots for private houses. In Nova Scotia, no Negro had been allowed to own land with direct access to the sea. In their determination not to suffer the same exclusion in Freetown, some people had hurriedly put up buildings near the shore and already owned jetties and boats. I am sure the reader will have no trouble imagining the outcry when Mr. Clarkson not only announced a decision to reserve the entire waterfront for the Company's own jetties and warehouses, but also ordered all who had built near the shore to move to plots further up the hill. In the end he gave in to the strong opposition and agreed to share the waterfront with the people already established there.

Junius Porter had witnessed the disturbance on that occasion. He was describing the scene in vivid terms when his face suddenly dissolved before my eyes and I swooned over my sewing. That was my last clear recollection for a whole week, for I, too, had become a victim of the deadly flux. I suffered agonies of griping pain, vomiting and severe purging; once again Felicia came to my rescue. She took leave from Mrs. Pepys to nurse me, and carried out her self-appointed task with a devotion I have never forgotten nor can ever repay. No sooner had I begun to take an interest in the world again, than she was ready to entertain me with the latest news and gossip.

'Whitefolk everywhere,' she said, the moment she sat down beside me on the porch one afternoon. 'Dey come wit' dere own ship.'

'Whitefolk! Where dey come from?' I asked.

'Junius say from one islan' up river dey call Bulama. Hey been go dere to make dey own place because dey don' want to live wit' darkies.'

'Enh! So why dey come to Freetown now?'

'To buy provision. Junius say mos' of dem done die; de ones left goin' back Englan'; dere leader one Dalrymple... Gov'nor refuse to sell to dem. He say provision not enough to share.'

'Good for him!' I said, disinclined to feel any sympathy for people who looked down on us. 'So what dey goin' do?'

Felicia chuckled. 'Junius say, when our own people know de whitefolk got plenty money dey buy extra provision an' sell to dem double price. But de storekeepers catch on quick and report to Gov'nor. Mr. Clarkson done close de store for now.'

'I pray God dey goin' go quick, before we suffer again.'

'I too prayin' for dat,' Felicia said.

Mr. Clarkson must have relented to some extent because the uninvited guests were still

134

among us when I was at last well enough to go for gentle strolls; but they sailed away soon afterwards and we were glad to be rid of them. It was also from Felicia that I learned that all the Councillors, except for Mr. Dawes, had been ordered by the Directors of the Company to return to England. Henceforth, Mr. Clarkson would be the sole Governor of Freetown, with William Dawes as his deputy.

'You tink anytin' goin' change?' I asked.

'Yes, Freetown goin' be differen' now,' Felicia said with conviction. 'Gov'nor Clarkson know how to coax people instead of cussin' and chidin' like dem other Councillor;...An' he done promise dat soon as de rain finish, Mr. Pepys goin' survey all de lan' an' everybody goin' get de firs' five acre of what day been promise.'

From what I witnessed when next I attended the compulsory worship service, Felicia's optimism was justified. The spirit of cheerfulness and cordiality made up for the still dreary weather outside, and instead of the lacklustre singing of previous months, the congregation praised The Almighty with joy. September ended, the month of October began, and the rains diminished at last, dwindling to short daily showers interspersed with several hours of dazzling sunshine. There continued to be thunderstorms at night, but they were short-lived and mild, for the most part. Gradually, the dark clouds disappeared, and with the clearing of the skies some of our troubles also ended. A supply ship arrived, laden with all the provisions we had lacked. Once again, our favourite foods filled the Company store - cheeses, ale, molasses, biscuits, salt beef and salt pork. For the first time in many weeks, I saw light at the end of the tunnel - a glimmer of hope that our new country might after all have more to offer than endless misery.

Chapter 15
Better days

The early weeks of the dry season brought air as fresh and as fragrant as if the world had newly been created; and there was much else to lift my spirits. Lush vegetation pushed its way through every bit of exposed soil; marvellous bursts of colour delighted my eyes at every turn— scarlet hibiscus, purple and pink bougainvillea, yellow allamanda bells, and white jasmine blossoms which added their heady fragrance to the other glories. Now that our Freetown had begun to assume the appearance of a proper town, I discovered that with the exception of my continuing dread of snakes, I no longer found our closeness to the forest a cause for anxiety. I delighted in the gorgeous butterflies and many lovely birds that frequented our back yard, and became especially fond of the little fellow, who greeted me each morning with a cheery trill that seemed to be saying,

'King's property, all correct.
King's property, all correct.'

One day I went out back to feed the six precious chickens for which Bro had given a Timmanee man one of our blankets. I was just outside the door, scattering grain, when all of a sudden a brilliant turquoise flash caught my eye among the shredding leaves of a banana tree. It was my first sight of a kingfisher. I had the pleasure of watching it for several seconds before it became aware of my presence and flew away.

Bro and Daniel changed the grass roof to one fashioned from palm fronds, tightly overlapping and neatly trimmed; and they extended the house to the back so that we now possessed private bedchambers, tiny though they were. In the idle hours of the rainy season, Daniel had discovered a talent for plaiting palm-fronds on a smaller scale to make serviceable mats; his handiwork now covered all the earthen floors, inspiring me to brighten the windows with yellow muslin curtains and, with the increased space in the house, to rearrange the furniture from Birchtown to my own satisfaction. There was as yet little to be seen by way of flowers or vegetables in the gardens Mammy had begun to plant before she left us, but some of the beautifully patterned leaves, which she had transplanted from the wild, had taken root and made a handsome display against the drab earth colour of the front wall. All in all, I felt a growing pride in our little home.

By this time, the streets had been named. The widest, appropriately named Broad Street ran the length of the waterfront on the northern side of Freetown. Two other thoroughfares ran from east to west and had been named Cross Street and Church Street. Nine shorter streets, of similar length and breadth, intersected the three wide thoroughfares, ascending the slope from the waterfront in the direction of the forest south of the town. Governor Clarkson named the short streets for the Directors of the Sierra Leone

Company and King George and Queen Charlotte of England; ours was Howe Street. We lived on the corner it formed with Church Street.

Jagged tree trunks still protruded here and there along the way, and the rains had caused an abundant resurgence of grass; but the streets were straight and wide, and though we took fine care not to stray beyond our boundaries, going for strolls became a favourite pastime. At the western-most point of Broad Street, a house for the Governor was under construction; other Company buildings had been completed towards the eastern end. We gained a fair picture of the plan of Freetown as we walked along the entire length of Broad Street and, by the power of imagination, could see that it might one day make us proud.

Meanwhile, a change had taken place in the composition of the population with the addition to our number of people from Granville Town - the first, ill-fated attempt to found a colony in Sierra Leone which Mr. Clarkson had mentioned in Nova Scotia. A few years before we arrived, King Jimmy and his warriors had burned the place to the ground following a dispute with the settlers, and the newcomers appeared to be what they were —rugged survivors of a catastrophe. To our surprise, many of them could speak the Timmanee language, and a few,were even known to have taken Timmanee women as their wives. For that reason, some of our own people kept them at arm's length when they first arrived; but with the passage of time they could no longer be distinguished from Nova Scotians.

Daniel befriended one of them, a certain Sam Perry who was a large young man with a deep voice and booming laugh. His slightly reddened eyes, and the wide gap between the upper two of his front teeth, gave him a rascally appearance which quite alarmed me at first. And besides, it was difficult to understand him, his version of the English tongue being somewhat different from our own. However, once we grew accustomed to his manner of speech, he provided us with wonderful entertainment from his storehouse of yarns. Sam Perry's tales often left me wide-eyed and gasping with amazement, or else shaking with laughter.

To hear him describe the burning of Granville Town was to smell the smouldering thatch, to experience the smarting eyes and to feel the hot breath of the fire on one's face. Apparently, King Jimmy gave them three days' warning of his intention to destroy their settlement, but like the people of Noah's time, many had thought it an empty threat. I recall another story Sam Perry told: how a slave ship once put down its anchor at their landing place and sailors came ashore in search of people to kidnap. Their quarries fled into the forest with the sailors in hot pursuit; all of a sudden, a huge ape appeared before them, baring his teeth and beating on his chest. Taken completely by surprise, the terrified sailors spun round and never stop running till they arrived panting on the jetty.

It was quite remarkable that Sam Perry and Daniel should have become close friends, the one so sparing of words, the other with a new yarn always ready on his lips. Besides, Sam Perry had no interest in hunting; fishing was his passion and he earned a fair living from that enterprise. Through his persuasion, Bro became a keen fisherman in his leisure hours and with this diversion at last began to cast aside his burden of grief. So relieved was I, that I gladly undertook the cleaning of his catch even when he brought it home after I thought I had completed my chores for the day. On occasion, I was occupied well into the night with the salting or smoking of fish.

There was another person captivated by Sam Perry, and that was Felicia Porter. Her hardy spirit must have recognised his own and reached out to it, for his appearance was of scant importance to her. The enchantment seemed to be mutual, which did not surprise me. Felicia was as entertaining as Sam Perry himself and as a result of better nourishment after the rainy season, and the freedom she now enjoyed, she had bloomed almost beyond recognition. It was still only when she smiled that her face could be described as beautiful, but her newly rounded cheeks and figure, and her saucy, hip- swaying walk caused many a male eye to turn in our direction when we went for a stroll.

It took some weeks for me to realise that Felicia and Sam Perry were keeping company together apart from the occasions when they met in my house. His name began to occur with great frequency in her conversation. It was, 'Sam say dis', and 'Sam say dat.' One Sunday afternoon, we went for a walk on the seashore by Susan's Bay, and as we wove a path through the small boys and youths whose favourite haunt it was, I asked her how it was between herself and Sam Perry; whether she had it in mind to marry him.

'Me, Felicia, marry a fisherman!' she exclaimed, 'an' was all my poor life cleanin' fish, saltin' fish, smokin' fish, till every part of me stinkin' of fish! God forbid! I happy how we be so Deannie, an' Sam happy too. He say, "Lissie", - he call me Lissie everytime - he say, "You de only woman for me. You don' ask me no plenty, plenty question, an' so I don' have to tell you no lie. When you don' see me, you don' fret. When you see me, you always glad."'

'But Licia,' I said, 'you don' want to born no children?'

'What children got to do wit' weddin'? If God give me children, I goin' love dem an' raise dem jus' de same if I done wed or not.'

'Licia, Mammy been say is wrong to born children if you not done wed. She been say only slave fit behave so.'

Felicia stopped and turned to face me, her expression unusually serious. After a moment she said,

'Deannie, you Mammy, God rest her soul, been a good, good woman. Since dat firs' day when I meet de two of you in Halifax, I been loves her like she my own Mammy. I tell her plenty tin' 'bout when I been in Saint John, but not one big tin' ... Nobody know 'bout dat, 'ceptin' Junius and Sam ... Deannie, Sam Perry not de firs' man I been wit' ... You know what I talkin' bout?'

I supposed her to mean that she had been 'carryin' on' with someone, but was too shy, and even afraid of what she might tell me, to ask her for greater enlightenment, so I simply nodded.

'You 'member, I tell you all 'bout dat man in Saint John, dat Mr. Cooper? Dat de man. He force heself on me, force heself on me ... After some time, I stop bleedin' every month, an' my belly gettin' big; he, too, see. After dat, he cuss me an' kick me more, so he woman not goin' tink is he been wit' me. He say he goin' sell me to West Indies plantation because he don' want for me to full he house wit' no nigger bastard. One day he kick me so hard I tumble down de step ... Praise God dat he kick me so! ... De baby born befo' time, poor tin' ; die de same day.'

Shocked to the core of my being by Felicia's revelation, I could only gasp her name in a horrified whisper.

'Don' look sorry so, girl,' she said, cheerfully chucking my chin. 'All dat done finish now ... Now Felicia Porter free. What Mr. Cooper take by force I givin' to Sam Perry for love sake. God lookin' inside my heart, Deannie. He know I not a bad girl.'

'Licia, I, too, knows dat, but de day Mammy die, like she know she goin' die dat same day, she make me to promise I never goin' born a baby 'less I done wed firs'.'

To my utter surprise, Felicia said firmly, 'You Mamm right, Deannie.'

'But jus' now you say..., ' I began.

'I says for me, not for everybody. You life an' my life not de same, Deannie. All de while you been get you Mammy an' Bro lookin' out for you. Dey done wed good an' proper. Dey been take you to church every week; everyday dey prayin' for you ...If you don' do what you been promise you Mammy, you never goin' be happy. You goin' be laughin' and dancin' an' singin', but here — inside you heart, you never goin' be happy ... You wait till you done wed, jus' like you Mammy say.' She added with a roguish smile, 'Not goin' be long now befo' somebody goin' snap you up quicker dan a dollar; ... an' I kin come dress you for de weddin'.'

'Oh, Licia,' I said, not feeling disposed to jest, 'no matter what you sayin' now, I knows one day you goin' fine one good man to marry to.'

'Maybe yes, maybe, no, but you not goin' catch Felicia Porter not sleepin' when night come because she worryin' 'bout not bein' wed ... It don' bother me none... True,' she said when I looked astonished.

Perhaps Mammy was turning in her grave as we spoke, but I admired Felicia more than ever that day - admired and envied her for having the courage, so lacking in me, to face up to life as it came, accepting any circumstances, taking the bitter with the sweet, the rough with the smooth, living one day at a time.

It was by now December, and Mr. Pepys was at last making progress with surveying the land to the east of East Street, and out on the slopes of St George's Hill behind the town. Nevertheless, very little land for farming had as yet been allocated. Bro complained almost daily about our, all but complete, dependence upon the Company for our livelihood and sustenance.

I had little cause for complaint myself, however. We had adequate shelter and were not in want. Both Bro and Daniel earned two shillings for a day's work and, since the cost of our weekly provisions usually amounted to no more than two dollars (about ten shillings), we were able to maintain a fair balance of credit at the Company store. With Daniel's hunting, my dressmaking and, of late, Bro's fishing, our means of livelihood and comfort had increased. Even my grief at the loss of Mammy had begun to subside. Pain still knifed through me from time to time, but more often now, fond memories of her left me smiling. Bro began to speak of her without tears and sighs; after some particular recollection he would say with pride, 'Deannie, you Mammy been a woman an' a half. You try an' be like her, you hear?'

It is too much to expect states of peace and contentment to endure this side of paradise. Once again, Fate must have looked down, decided the Dixon family showed signs of too much contentment, and took steps to change that situation.

Chapter 16
A narrow escape and Governor Clarkson departs

It was sometimes Daniel's practice when out hunting, to be away from home throughout the night; but when Bro and I returned from an early morning service one day in December and he still had not returned, I became uneasy. I began the day's tasks and was tossing grain to the chickens when I heard cries of, 'Lord, have mercy! Lord, have mercy!' coming from the street. I ran round to the front of the house and saw a small crowd approaching, in the midst of it, a man carrying someone on his back. My thoughts raced to the still absent Daniel and, to my horror, saw that the man's burden was indeed my brother, barely recognisable under a mask of thick, clotted blood.

'Bro!' I shrieked, 'Bro! Bro!' not realising that my father was already pushing his way through the crowd from which questions, answers, and comments were coming in quick succession.

'Let we carry him inside de house?'

'No, carry him straight to Dr. Winterbottom house.'
'He done die? He done die?'

'No, he breathin'.'

'What happen?'

'Lord, have mercy!'

Frantic with fear, I sped before the crowd, wailing unashamedly all the way down to Broad Street where the new Company doctor lived, and once I arrived at his house I banged so loudly at the door that he had vexation writ large on his face when he opened it.

'What is it this time, pray?' he asked. 'You people are forever in a panic about one thing or another.'

'Oh, Doctor, Doctor,' I sobbed, 'is my broda. He face all over blood... He goin' die if you don' do sometin' quick. He not able to talk even.'

My distress must have appealed to Dr. Winterbottom's better nature, for though he still wore a scowl as he shut the door in my face, he reappeared with his bag of instruments when he heard the noise of the approaching crowd. James Collier, another hunter, was the man carrying Daniel; he laid him at the doctor's feet.

'Pray, stand back! Stand back, I say!' Dr. Winterbottom ordered, as he went down to his knees to examine Daniel's wound.

'My faith! this was caused by a bullet!' he exclaimed. 'How in the name of heaven did such a thing come to pass?'

'It was me done it, Sir,' James Collier con-fessed and almost weeping with remorse, gave an account of how the accident occurred as Dr. Win-terbottom went to work with swabs and a needle..

He had been on his way home, feeling dis-couraged after a night of fruitless hunting, when he heard movements among trees close to his path. So eager was he to kill any manner of game that instead of pausing to consider what had caused the movements, he fired straight into bush. To his consternation, he heard an all too human yell, and Daniel stumbled out, clutching his bleeding face.

The bullet had torn off the tip of his right ear and sliced across his cheek, exposing his jaw-bone in a gaping wound. I had to turn away as Dr. Winterbottom brought the lips of the wound to-gether and closed them with stitches. Daniel would never again be my well-favoured brother, but we were thankful when Dr. Winterbottom as-sured us that, with careful nursing, he would live. It was almost Christmas before he was fully restored to health, for the wound festered, giving him a high fever. For many days and nights he tossed and moaned and muttered in delirium; I believe he would have perished but for his own strong constitution, the herb poultices supplied by Sister Sophia, and our frequent and fervent prayers. By the time his fever broke, I was ex-hausted in body and mind after sleepless nights and anxious days, but felt proud of myself nevertheless; I had played, with success, what would have been Mammy's role.

During the days of Daniel's illness there was always someone keeping us company in the afternoons and evenings, either Felicia, or Junius, Sam Perry, or Sister Sophia from across the street. If my memory serves me well, it was Junius who, during one of these visits, mentioned that Governor Clarkson would shortly be returning to England on leave.

'So is Dawes goin' be in charge, eh?' Bro said gloomily (the Governor's deputy was well respected but, apparently, not well liked).

'You mark what I say,' he continued in the same doom laden voice. 'Jus' now we goin' get trouble here again.'

Most of Freetown assembled on the wharf on the day Governor Clarkson sailed away, which event took place on the thirtieth day of December. In his parting remarks, he gave assurances that farming plots would be ready for allocation in two weeks, appealed to us to support Mr. Dawes until his return, then read out such a lengthy prayer that, as he went on and on, I remember thinking that he was telling God everything else he wished us to hear before his departure.

Printed copies of that prayer were later distributed to every household; to this day, we, the founders of Freetown, consider it almost sacred - especially, the following words:

'Should any person have a wicked thought in his heart or do anything to disturb the peace and comfort of our Colony, let him be rooted out, O, God, from the face of the earth, but have mercy on him hereafter.'

At the time, we thought our beloved Governor would be absent for no more that a few months, but it was still with warmth and sadness that we bade him farewell. As Bro had predicted, Governor Clarkson's ship was hardly out of sight when trouble started again. One evening, early in January, he stormed into the house after the day's work with the news that Mr. Dawes had ordered Mr. Pepys to postpone laying out the farms and concentrate on fortifying the Company's cotton plantation which had been established to the east of Freetown.

'Is Scotia again!' Bro raged. 'Dey goin' delay an' make excuse, delay an' make excuse, an' we not goin' get notin' day done promise we. Dem Company people knows if dey give we lan' we be workin' for weself an' dey not goin' get dey cheap labour no more.'

I did my best to calm him, but it was no easy task. He would subside, then burst out again with clenched fists,

'Oh, God! when dis slavery goin' finish? When?'

Being young and without responsibilities or ambitions myself, I was more concerned about safety than farm land, especially since I was still somewhat fearful of the Timmanees. As recently as the Christmas just passed, a crowd of them had arrived in the town dancing and singing and drumming behind one of their number robed in dyed grass from his neck down to his ankles, and with his entire head hidden by a horrible carved mask. We heard that they went down to the Company store demanding rum and became quite hostile when they learnt that it would not be opened that day. On another occasion, I had been down by Susan's Bay when a party of their war canoes passed by heading for King Jimmy's town. They had waved their oars and yelled at us in a way that made me shudder. For that reason, though I understood Bro's dissatisfaction, I was secretly relieved to learn that more fortifications were to be built.

We had discovered December and January to be the favourite months for the arrival of slavers in search of human cargo; and never could we understand why Company officials, supposedly loathing the slave trade, allowed them to water their ships in our harbour. Since fear frays the nerves and frayed nerves lead to ill-temper, Freetown was a turbulent place in the first weeks of 1793. Quarrels and fights broke out on the slightest provocation, keeping the constables and town marshalls busy. Mr. Dawes had to administer several public floggings and, as a result, decided to make sweeping changes to the way Freetown was governed.

To assist the constables and town marshalls maintain law and order, every year every ten families would elect what he called a Tything-man. Every ten Tythingmen would elect a Hundredor who would serve as a junior magistrate with authority to try petty cases. Only male adults, white as well as black, were eligible for election to these positions, but all adults had the vote. The creation of Hundredors and Tythingmen boosted the low morale in Freetown, and Mr. Dawes might have weathered this stormy period had not a certain Zachary Macaulay arrived to serve as his deputy. He was a young man, not yet thirty, it was said, but with his stern countenance, looked far older than his years.

Zachary Macaulay proved to be a high-handed type of individual; once convinced that his opinions were justified, he tolerated no opposition. He strengthened Mr. Dawes's arm and together they decreed that those who had not yet received their farm land would have to wait until all fortification work was complete. Since this contradicted Governor Clarkson's assurances before his departure, it caused another ferocious outcry. To make matters worse, they also decreed that those who had erected buildings near the waterfront should remove themselves forthwith; plots of land within five hundred feet of the water would, in future, be reserved solely for the use of the Company.

On the very evening of the Governor's decree, the recently elected Hundredors invited all adults to attend a meeting at the church to discuss the situation. I was extremely proud when Bro said that I was old enough to attend if I so desired since I would attain fifteen years of age that May.

From the beginning, it was a tumultuous gathering. Loud, angry voices tried to speak at once so that nothing could be heard except a roar. Brother Luke Jordan, one of the Methodist Pastors, presided over the deliberations. He had to bang on the table at which he sat before achieving a measure of quiet. Into the midst of this hubbub stepped Mr. Pepys, sent by the Governor to inquire about the cause of the disturbance.

'Is because Gov'nor an' Mr. Macaulay don disturb' we,' was Pastor Jordan's angry reply. 'De Company cheatin' we. You people bring we here wit' lie. Dey been promise we freedom. We lan' dey not give we till now, an' today Gov'nor givin' we order like we still slave.'

At this, angry shouts erupted. When Mr Pepys indicated that he wished to say something, several more minutes passed before Pastor Jordan could quieten the crowd enough for the Governor's messenger to speak.

'I do not know why you people are agitating like this,' Mr. Pepys said. 'Not one of you is entitled to a single square foot of land unless it be given to you by the Company. All this area - from Susan's Bay to St George's Bay - all of it was purchased not not by you but by the Company. It belongs to the Company, not to you.'

'Gov'nor Clarkson been promise we twenty acre!' was the cry. 'An' he say we kin share de waterfront.'

'If that is true, he must have been intoxicated when he made such promises; he had no authority to do so ... In any event, Mr. Clarkson will not be returning to Freetown. Mr. Dawes is now the Governor and his decisions are final... I therefore advise you to go home quietly and cause no further trouble.'

Deeply upset by the news that our beloved Mr. Clarkson would not be returning, and by the suggestion that he might ever have spoken or acted under the influence of liquor, tempers flared again. Several hotheads jumped to their feet and shook their fists at Mr Pepys, screaming,

'Go 'way! Go 'way befo' we finish you. Fancy talkin' 'bout a good an' godly man like dat. Go 'way!'

Without another word, Mr. Pepys took his leave; Pastor Jordan banged on the table with his gavel. Pastor Cato Perkins of the Countess of Huntingdon's Connexion, now rose to speak.

'Slavery so much in we blood still for we to 'gree let dem people trample on we so? ... If de lan' belong to de Company, so what'? If not for we, dere goin' be no Freetown.'

Amid shouts of agreement, he went on, 'I kin wager anytin', even my life, dem Director in Englan' don' know what goin' on here. Thomas Peters, God rest his soul, been say dey is God-fearin' people. If dey hear 'bout it, dey not goin' like it one bit. Is dem two is drunk, Dawes an' Macaulay. Dey drunk wit' power!'

'You done said it, Broda!' someone shouted, causing an outburst of laughter so that once again, Pastor Jordan found it difficult to restore order. I did not know the name of the grey-haired man who next rose to his feet. His indignation made him stutter, unless that was his usual manner of speech.

'We don' have no place to work 'ceptin' Company work. Any work dey like dey kin give we; pay we anytin' dey want pay we ... Work fit for slave is only what dey give mos' all of we to do — diggin', diggin' de whole time. Let dey give we de lan' so if we dig, we goin' be diggin' for we-self, not for no master.'

Thunderous applause followed his remarks; Pastor Jordan spoke again.

'You all 'member what we late broda, Thomas Peters been do when he not satisfy wit' we situation? Let we act like him, brodas an' sisters. Let we sen' to dem Director an' tell dem how dey treatin' we here.'

Wild enthusiasm greeted t h i s s u gg e s t i o n.   Straightaway, it was decided to hold an election to choose two delegates who would travel to England with the complaint. Pastor Cato Perkins was elected and also one Brother Isaac Anderson. The meeting ended late, yet the Hundredors and Tythingmen remained behind to draft the petition to be presented to the Directors in England.

From that day on, and during the ensuing months, relations between settlers and the Company officials became decidedly unfriendly. There was a man called Perry Turner who lived with his family at the top of East Street. His was the last house before the boundary. One morning he received a notification from Governor Dawes that the plot on which his house stood was required for building a fortification. Perry Turner ignored the letter. The next day, Governor Dawes requested his presence in his chambers to explain himself. According to Daniel, Perry Turner told the Governor that he had no intention of giving up the house he had built with much sweat and toil over a year. The Governor sent Company officials to evict him, but Perry Turner still refused to leave his house, and his neighbours pelted the officials with the filthiest garbage they could lay their hands on. The Company officials finally gave up the attempted eviction and hurried away, followed by a jeering crowd. They passed our house and, having run outside to see what the commo-

tion was about, curiosity made me decide to accompany them; but I kept to the fringes of the mob, for that is what it was
becoming.

By the time we reached the gates of the Governor's house, the crowd was about a hundred strong and rowdy in the extreme. People jostled the officials when they tried to open the gates, pressing so closely around them that they had no alternative but to leave them open. We all surged into the Governor's yard, with the ringleaders yelling,

'Where dat Dawes? Let he come an' face we! Let we see he ugly face!'

The Governor himself appeared then and, with remarkable courage, I thought, faced the angry mob.

'What do you people want?' he shouted in an equally furious voice.

'We want let you leave we in peace!'

'An' give we we lan'.'

'You will receive your land in due course; there are other considerations more important.'

'We want we lan' now! Now! Now!' chanted the crowd; one voice added,

'You people tinkin' 'bout profit all de time; you don' care 'bout we.'

'Give we de lan'!'

'Let we burn everytin' down!' another voice yelled.

'Aye! Aye! Let we burn de house down!'
'All right, all right, all right,' Governor Dawes shouted. 'It seems you will not give me your support and I cannot force you. You are not prisoners here. You are free men.'

'So why you not treatin' we like free men?'

Ignoring the question, he replied, 'You are not behaving like people who can reason. All the orders I make are for your own benefit as well as the Company's. You are behaving like children - blind and deaf to all but your own desires. Obviously, it is time for me to depart from this place.'

'Go! Go! Go!' many voices cried.

'Who been ask you to come here?'

Governor Dawes slammed his door in our faces. The uproar continued for some minutes longer, but no acts of violence were committed. Gradually the noise died down, and we dispersed. Later that day, we discussed the matter at home. Bro said,

'Trouble wit' dat man, he don' understan' we. Most of we here been born slave an' we hate to be slave. Den when we run way to be free, dem whitefolk make promise and dey not keep dey promise. So when whitefolk here talkin' like dey we master, an' make like dey lookin' to break dey promise again, we boun' to feel vexation. Not so?...You see, Gov'nor Clarkson, he a man who always he keep de Lord before him, so he know how to talk to people. He always courteous when he makin' order; an' when he got to give we bad news, he himself look so sorry, we sorry for him an' we ready to help him.'

I pointed out that the Governor had not been so meek and mild over the Thomas Peters affair.

'Well, you kin blame him, when it look like-ungratefulness?' Bro replied, 'but let we talk 'bout Dawes again. If he not change he way, mark what I sayin', if he not change he way, he not goin' be here for long.'

The Governor changed neither his decisions nor his ways and the dissatisfaction in Freetown continued to be the main topic of conversation at home, after church, in the street, just every-where. Throughout our second rainy season he and Zachary Macaulay continued to anger people in one way or another, going so far as to water the rum; many of the petty officials took their cue from them.

I experienced this change of attitude myself when I went down to the Company store to purchase our provisions one morning. For some weeks I had realised that prices were rising; the price of salt pork, for one thing, had risen from ten pence a pound to two shillings a pound. I made bold to comment on this and the tally clerk, a whey-faced, young man called Mr. Tulloch, responded with a scowl instead of the pleasant countenance with which he once carried out his duties.

'This is the Company's price. Take it or leave it.'

For the sake of maintaining good relations, he could have told me why the prices had to rise; that it was on account of the scarcity of all commodities brought about by England's war with France. It was only after I complained about his conduct that Felicia gave me that explanation which she had overheard in the home of her employers.

'Dey say, Englan' fightin' dem French people because day done kill dey king. Dat why food scarce an' dear so. Every tin' for soldiers now.'

That November, there occurred an incident which showed clearly the extent of ill-will towards the Company. I was sitting by the window plaiting my hair when I heard desperate cries of 'Fire!' and the Company bell began a wild clanging. With half my hair plaited and the other half standing on end as if I had lost my reason, I dashed towards the waterfront from whence the alarm came. Through thick swathes of smoke an awful sight met my eyes. A ship was ablaze on the water and it was as if brimstone had come up from hell. Even from a distance of two hundred yards, it was possible to hear cracking and crashing as her timbers burned. From the landing place and in small boats, Company officials were making desperate but futile efforts to control the blaze, and this was the observation that shocked me: the crowd that had gathered to watch the conflagration lifted not a finger to assist them. Indeed, some laughed and made rude remarks about the officials' frantic efforts. As the charred skeleton of the ship finally sank, one man even shouted, 'Oh, Judgement Day! Where all dey profit now, eh?'

Not understanding how anyone could rejoice in the face of such a disaster, I slunk away as soon as the ship went down, feeling somewhat ashamed to have been among the gloaters. That fire could have been heaven's judgement on the Company, but we all suffered as a result of it because the stricken vessel had been none other than the Company's store ship, the York. A few weeks later, another fire broke out, this time on land. It swept towards us from the east end of Cross Street but mercifully burned itself out before reaching our house. Several people lost their homes and who could talk about judgement then? Indeed, on the Sunday following that second disaster, Pastor George preached on a text: 'For who hath known the mind of the Lord?' Those in the congregation who had rejoiced at the Company's loss must have squirmed in their seats.

Shortly afterwards, Governor Dawes's health broke down under the strain of the trying climate and the stresses of trying to govern where he knew himself to be hated. As Bro had predicted, before the new year was far advanced, he was obliged to return to England, a wreck of the man who had succeeded Governor Clarkson with such confidence. Zachary Macaulay now became the acting Governor and the days of successful defiance were at an end. In that young man, our people met a formidable opponent

Chapter 17
My first suitor

It was the month of May, 1794, and once again a rainy season was almost upon us. I was now sixteen years old and having managed our home for two years, considered myself a grown woman. As if to prove my proud opinion of myself justified, a suitor for my hand appeared. He was a pastor-in-training whom I shall call Prince Godfrey. I first realised his warm feelings towards me during the Whitsun koonking because he was excessively attentive and always endeavoured to secure a place by my side when we formed a circle to dance. When Bro said it was time to leave the festivity, Prince Godfrey expressed such disappointment that it was no surprise when Bro, looking well pleased, told me that he had given the young man permission to call.

Prince Godfrey had somehow acquired more book learning than any of the men of my acquaintance, and there was no doubt that marriage to a pastor would raise my status in the community. However, though somewhat flattered to be the object of his affections I was less than eager to become his wife, the reason being that, as a man, Prince Godfrey held little charm for me. For one thing, he was many years my senior, more than ten in my estimation, below average in height and with a tendency towards stoutness. For another thing, though his cinnamon coloured skin was smooth as a baby's, he had a proud look which repelled me. Worst of all, he walked in a fussy, short stepped manner, sticking out his rear end like the tail-feathers of a cock. How could I contemplate marrying a man whose progress down the street never failed to make me giggle?

He paid me his first formal visit one Sunday afternoon. The moment he appeared, Bro, who had been sitting with me on the porch, rose hastily to greet him. Clearly, my father harboured no doubts as to Prince Godfrey's worthiness as a suitor for his daughter, for no sooner had he offered him a seat than he declared himself smitten with a headache and obliged to retire to bed.

Prince Godfrey rested his plump hands on his plump knees. First he beamed at me, then astonished me by speaking the kind of English nobody, not even the most learned among us spoke, except on formal occasions such as church services with Holy Communion.

'Well, Sister Deannie,' he said, his eyes warm upon my face, 'permit me to say your appearance at church this morninggave me much pleasure...Charming, very charming indeed. Them good Lord created the colour pink just for you.'

Responding with a timid smile, I offered to fetch him a dish of tea.

'Presently, Sister Deannie, presently;...just now, I do believe all the refreshment I require is here by my side.'

I dropped my eyes to avoid the growing ardour in his gaze; he chuckled at my bashfulness.

'I see you are a modest maiden; admirable... most admirable. We have to endure too many brazen hussies in this place — women who are an abomination before the Lord.'

As he continued to speak, his voice rose as if he would use me to practise a sermon...'An abomination and a disgrace to their womanhood ... Women like that deserve to be flogged.'

'Flogged, Broda Godfrey?' I asked with a gasp.

'Yes, indeed,' he replied in the same tone. 'Whipped like disobedient children to remind them that the Lord created woman from Adam's rib, not the other way around. No woman should seek to dominate a man... especially when he is her husband. It is against the will of the Lord!'

Not knowing how to respond, I simply gazed at him. He dropped his voice to a murmur as soft as a kitten's fur.

'You are different, Sister Deannie. I can see that your dear mother, God rest her soul, bred you to be a true Christian woman - gentle and modest and sweet.'

Without warning, he laid his hand upon my skirt and fondled my knee, making me rise as abruptly as if stung by a wasp. Muttering that I must make some tea, I pushed my way past him into the house. I was still inwardly shaken when I returned, whereas my suitor looked the picture of complacent ease with his hands clasped upon his knees.

My feelings of confident womanhood had vanished with the realisation that I knew of no way to rebuff Prince Godfrey's advances, short of undignified flight. As I nervously handed him his tea and resumed my seat, I dearly wished another person would come to call; but I need not have been so apprehensive, for he said at once,

'Pray, forgive me, Sister Deannie ... I meant no dishonour to you; all of a sudden your comeliness overwhelmed me.'

Since I remained silent, he changed the subject and asked in the manner of a pastor visiting a member of his flock whether it was my practice to read the Bible.

'I do not refer to reading verses at family prayers, but reading it by yourself; just you and the Lord.'

Pleased with the turn the conversation had taken, I replied,

'Yes, Broda Godfrey, but not every day... I alone got to go to de store, to clean de house, to wash de clothes, cook, see to de garden, den I got to sew, an' sometimes to clean fish... When evenin' come I fit only to lay me down an' sleep.

'I understand, I understand,' he said easily, 'but I would ask that you make a greater effort, Sister Deannie; perhaps wake up at an earlier hour. The woman I take to wife must be a perfect Christian in every respect;...you are aware that I wish to make you my wife?'

'I guessed it,' was my reluctant reply.

'Yes, Sister Deannie, I wish to make you my wife.'

'But I too young to wed, Broda Godfrey.'

'Too young? Never! Look around you ... Many maidens of fewer years than yours are already wed. Believe me, you are ripe for marriage. '

Accompanied by another look of excessive admiration, those words made me shrink into my chair once more, fearing another unwelcome caress. To my relief, Prince Godfrey merely said,

'I have been advised that the fairer sex often deem it unfitting to accept a proposal of marriage when first it is received. However, I must tell you that you will not find a better man than me for a girl of your quality in this place; not if you wait till judgement day ... Most of these other fellows are scum − illiterate or half-illiterate ruffians. You need a man who can give you the decent and sober life your dear mother would have wished for you ... Forgive me if I seem to boast, but I speak of a man like myself, Sister Deannie - upright, God-fearing... As my wife you will be able to improve yourself; to become with me a leader in the church and in the community ... When can I expect an answer?'

That demand came so suddenly that I could only stammer, 'S ... soon, Broda Godfrey.'

'I swear, you will not regret it if you agree to become my wife ... I have great prospects ... great prospects.'

The rest of our conversation was in that vein so that by the time Prince Godfrey took his leave, I had to boil up the kettle and drink another dish of tea to soothe my nerves. In my heart, I knew that I would not find happiness in marriage with a man like him, though in my inexperience of the different characters of men at the time, I could not have explained wherein his own so repelled me. Only in later years did I give it the label of self- conceit, with a touch of the tyrant as well.

Later that evening, Bro sought to know my thoughts about the matter. The look on my face must have told him all he needed to know, but he made no attempt to press Prince Godfrey's suit, no doubt hoping that in time I would change my mind. Only to Felicia did I confide my true opinion of my suitor. She laughed and laughed at my account of his visit then, having wiped away tears, grew serious all at once.

'Deannie, how 'bout Junius? ' she said. 'He tink you de finest girl in de whole place. All dis time I been tellin' him you too small ... but now you bigger, an' men comin' courtin' ...How 'bout him,...Hmm?'

Such was my surprise that I exclaimed, 'Junius! Licia, Junius like my broda , jus' like you my sista.' Felicia directed her straightest gaze at me. 'Dat de only reason, Deannie?' She asked, and before I could answer, went on, 'No, don' say notin' more... I knows what you tinkin' ... Junius an' me don' have book learnin' like you and Daniel. Junius kin read lil' bit now, but he don' talk so fine, eh? Not like dat preacher-man. '

'Licia, is not dat.'

'Yes, is dat. Let me tell you, girl, book learnin' not so wonderful, else why you not say yes to dat man even befo' de word out of he mouth? Why you an' me laughin' at him jus' now?... I goin' tell you why. Is because wit' all he book learnin' an' pretty talkin' an' preachin' an' all, he don' warm you blood one bit ... Inside you heart you know dat when you tinkin' 'bout weddin' you want a man who goin' warm more dan jus' you head; somebody who goin' keep you warm all over when de rain comin' down, or when de smokes blowin' col' in January.'

'Oh, Licia,' I said, laughing helplessly.

'Is true, Deannie! Junius got no book learnin' but he not a fool; you kin help him. An he young an' strong ; God willin' you not goin' be left a widow befo' you done ol' ... You two kin work an' grow ol' side by side ... An' Deannie, Junius kin give you so much lovin'- lovin' you never knows was in dis worl' ... An' then you goin' be my true, true sister.'

'Licia, if Junius say he like my face, dat don' mean to say he want me an' him to wed. You know he always jestin'. Anytime I meet him he jus' wink he eye to me an' say, "How Sister Deannie doin' today?" or sometin' like dat. He never talk anytin' serious. An' when he come to call is to talk to Bro or Danny.'

'If dat what you been tinkin' all dis time, you got no sense in you head, Deannie Dixon. Junus comin' to you house to see you. He don' want Bro to say he not good enough for you if he tell him he want to come courtin', so he jus' come like is you all he visitin', but I know he hopin' ... If he believe you like him, Deannie, he goin' make bol' an' ask Bro for you ... So what you say?... Let I tell him you willin'?'

'Licia, I don' know,' I replied. 'I never done tink 'bout Junius so.'

'Well, start tinkin' 'bout him now; ... but I not goin' say notin' to him 'ceptin' you tell me to.'

And so I began to consider Junius Porter. The next time he stopped by our house, I gave him my fullest attention while he conversed with Bro, and thus discovered that he was more well favoured than I had ever thought him, though, his comeliness lay not in his face, which was rather long and bony, but in his well shaped hands, his light brown eyes, his bronze complexion and the grace with which he moved. I continued my secret observation as the weeks passed, and felt that I could love him; indeed, I had ceased to think of him as my second brother. Yet, I was still reluctant to accept him as a suitor. I feared disappointing Bro who, I knew, would want me to marry a man with at least a trade, whereas Junius was still employed as a general labourer. On the other hand, I had by now discovered that my father would take in good part any decision I might make in this regard, for when I finally summoned the courage to tell him that I had no desire to wed Prince Godfrey, he merely said,

'Deannie, if I say I not disappoint', I not goin' be talkin' true; but I never goin' force you to marry nobody. Me an' you Mammy been pick weself to wed; so when you ready, you pick you own man ... Only tin' I say is I hope you don' take up wit' one dem Granville Town men like you frien', Licia. Dey look too rough for my lil girl.'

Nevertheless, I could not decide and, as a consequence, a visit from Junius Porter became an occasion for inward agitation hidden with carefree laughter.

Meanwhile, the delegates had returned from England with troubling news. They had been thoroughly humiliated over there. The directors had delayed meeting them for as long as possible without dismissing them outright. When, at last, they finally agreed to see them, it was only to express absolute confidence in the Governor and to appeal to them to give the Company their full support and loyalty. With his arm thus strengthened, acting Governor Macaulay paid scant attention to any more murmurs of discontent. Prices continued to rise as the war between England and France continued, but that was not the only reason for bad tempers in Freetown. In addition to the old complaints, Zachary Macaulay was looked upon with deep suspicion because he seemed far too friendly with the captains of the slave ships that continued to visit Freetown. Rumour had it that he even entertained them in his house and that he was planning to sell all the troublemakers back into slavery in the West Indies. Freetown became a pile of kindling awaiting a flame; sure enough, the flame was lit.

A certain slaver called Grierson, came to water his ship and became involved in a dispute with one of our people who worked on the wharf - a man called Robert Keeling. We heard that Grierson had insulted Robert Keeling, declaring that he deserved to be whipped for insolence to his superior. Like the free man he considered himself to be, Robert Keeling heaped abuse on Grierson in his turn and, with another man called Scipio Channel, had all but assaulted him. Grierson reported the matter to the Governor who, without further investigation, promptly dismissed Robert Keeling and Scipio Channel for disrespecting a white man.

In past conflicts between our people and Company officials the other inhabitants of Freetown had taken little active part. Law-abiding for the most part, like me, the majority wished only to carry on with their own affairs in peace. Despite much grumbling in private, and attending settler meetings when summoned, they usually left the high dramas to the belligerent few - those to whom Pastor George frequently referred as, 'the generation of vipers'. But we were sensitive to our position as former slaves and children of former slaves; such prejudice in favour of a slave-trader was, therefore, not to be meekly borne or taken lightly. On this occasion, all but the most passive among us were roused to indignation. Bro, who had been elected a Tythingman earlier that year, was called to attend a hastily summoned meeting of the Nova Scotian officials. He returned from it raging with frustration and anger.

'We gone to tell Macaulay dat we tink he wrong to dismiss dem two men befo' he 'done give dem proper hearin' an' to take up for dat slave captain so. De man refuse to listen even. Instead he holler on we like we is children, an' say we got no right to tell him what he fit do ... What dey been make we Hundredor an' Tythingman for, eh? ... What power we got? ... What freedom we got? What dis name Freetown mean?... Only freedom we got is what Macaulay feel to give we ... Praise God you Mammy done go to de Lord befo' dis day!'

When he grew calmer, he said, 'Daniel, Bible done tell we deliverance goin' come from God. What dat mean?... Black people got to be in chain till kingdom come? Is God done give white-folk dis yoke to wear on we neck, an' we got to bear it till God heself take it away? ... How long!'

'Bro it don' mean dat at all,' Daniel said. 'It mean we got to fight for weself, den God goin' help we.'

Bro shook his grey head sadly. ' I don' know notin' no more.'

The next morning, Daniel burst into the house soon after he and Bro had set out for their day's work. He had come to tell me that under no circumstances was I to venture down to Broad Street because riots had broken out.

'Dey fightin' down to Gov'nor yard an' Crankapone an' dem constable not able to stop de crowd. Dey say if he arrest anybody dey goin' string him up.'(Richard Crankapone who had walked with Junius and Felicia from Saint John to Halifax was now the town marshall).

'All de whitefolk carryin' gun an' dey done put a cannon befo' de Gov'nor gate; people beat-in' up anybody supportin' de Gov'nor, an' dey sayin' all Baptist support de Gov'nor, so you stay here, you hear?'

'But Danny, how 'bout you and Bro? Dey knows you is Baptist an' you own face don' hide wit' dat great big scar!'

'Don' trouble you mine for me, Deannie, I kin look out for meself.'

Before I could utter another word of protest, or ask what had become of Bro, he was gone.

All that day, the rioting never stopped. Confined to our yard as I was, hearing musket shots, shouts and screams, I became terrified for the safety of Bro and Daniel, especially when I remembered the sight of Daniel's bloodied face after his accident. When they eventually returned, I burst into tears of relief, at the same time scolding them for scaring me out of my wits. And the rioting continued. Even when we retired for the night, hours passed before I stopped hearing shouts and shots in the distance.

The next day, a Sunday, our usual clangorous summons to church rang through the town. Still law- abiding at heart, Bro answered the summons and allowed me to accompany him. Daniel, however, refused to attend. It seemed that no Methodists had answered the summons either, for the large hall was half empty. We realised this would not be a regular service when we observed a Company official standing at the lectern instead of the Company chaplain. When he decided that no one else was coming, he began to read out a long message from the Governor..

The first part of it was quite cordial. Governor Macaulay reminded us that without Company rule we would be at the mercy of slave-traders;

that they would surely seek to capture young people and transport them to the West Indies for sale. He reminded us that we would also be at the mercy of the Timmanees who, by sheer weight of numbers, would make us lose all we had gained of education and civilisation. He went on to say that God would take vengeance on us for ingratitude if we continued to act in so stubborn a manner, but that if we would only be patient, the war with France would presently come to an end and most of the reasons for our complaints would cease to exist.

That was as far as friendliness went. The second part of the message informed us that a brig, the Venus, now at anchor in the harbour, would be put at the disposal of any settlers who wished to return to Nova Scotia. Meanwhile, there would be an investigation into the riots. Until then, the Company stores would remain closed and all workers put on suspension, and so on and so forth.

'Dat man broda to Satan,' Daniel said in his quiet way, when we told him what had transpired.

'You done talk de true word,' Bro agreed. 'Zachary Macaulay crafty like Satan ... He done study we well, an' he not got a good Christian heart like Gov'nor Clarkson. He know we 'fraid of slavery, we 'fraid of Timmanee people an' we 'fraid of God. Right? So he scared we wit' all tree. Till now dey not give we we groun', so we got no livin' 'ceptin' wit' de Company; so what he do? He take away we livin' till we promise to be good children. Den he say if we don' like Freetown we kin go back to Scotia. He know full well nobody don' want to go back to no Scotia...What we got here now is town slavery, an' notin' we kin do 'bout dat.'

Thus was peace of a kind restored. Many people were thrown into jail; three women were publicly flogged which, must have pleased Prince Godfrey. Eight ring-leaders, including Scipio Channel and Robert Keeling were sent to England for trial; seven other settlers agreed to go as witnesses against them. This last created a conflict in my mind. Time and time again, Pastor George had told us that it was our Christian duty to obey those set in authority over us. These eight ringleaders had committed a sin by leading a riot against the Company and therefore deserved to be put on trial. The conflict in my mind concerned the seven who had agreed to bear witness against them. Bro said it was their Christian duty to tell the truth in court about what happened; Daniel said they deserved to be shunned when they returned to Freetown. I was inclined to agree with him, though I kept my opinion to myself.

By mid-August the rainy season was once again upon us in full force, quenching the emotional fires of the preceding months. We huddled in our miserable dwellings, suffering from damp and hunger, praying for God's mercy to help us to stay alive. In the end, the Governor banished the eight ringleaders of the riots to fend for themselves, and banned lesser offenders from ever again working for the Company. By those actions Zachary Macaulay made it clear that the will of the Company could never be challenged with any hope of success; trying to do so would only incur severe punishment. He had the people of Freetown right where he wanted them — under his thumb.

My own life was no less unsatisfactory. Having no idea of my changing feelings towards him, Junius Porter continued to pay us regular visits and to jest with me in his usual manner, never by word or look revealing that he desired a closer bond with me. Indeed, I began to wonder whether Felicia had not been mistaken; whether, being so fond of me herself, it was she and not her brother who hoped for our union. How I longed for Mammy then.

I have often wondered how long the matter would have remained thus undecided had not a great upheaval forced us to put away all pretence and fear of wounded pride or future regret. On the twenty-eighth day of September, 1794, a French fleet attacked Freetown with cannon fire. Armed sailors came ashore, and in a matter of days had destroyed the work of nearly three years of sweat and toil.

Chapter 18
Freetown is destroyed

The attack came on a Sunday morning, at the time when most people were attending church services. I was at home, having barely recovered from another bout of fever. After almost a week of enforced seclusion, it was with great enjoyment that I was sitting in the yard basking in the sunlight like a happy lizard and revelling in my little flower garden which was in full bloom. Oh, it felt good to be alive and to have once again survived a rainy season! My sense of well-being made me forget all my anxieties; I hugged myself with a sigh of deep contentment as I glanced idly towards the water. To my utter surprise, I observed a fleet of seven or eight large vessels sailing around the part of town known as Falconbridge Point. I remember wondering what ships they could be, for though there were always ships in the harbour, it was unusual for them to arrive in such numbers and all at once. But I felt not the slightest hint of alarm. They were a beautiful sight against the clear blue of the sky and added to my delight.

Several minutes passed; then an explosion shattered the quiet of the morning. At first I took it to be the start of one of the thunderstorms frequent at that time of year and peered curiously at the sky. For a few minutes it remained as cloudless as before. Then the sound came again - and again, echoing from the hills with too much regularity to be mistaken any longer for thunderclaps. I also observed that in the direction of the waterfront thick clouds of smoke had begun to obscure the sky. A smell, not unlike vinegar, drifted towards me and as I wrinkled my nose, it struck me that what I was hearing was cannonfire. Just then, I saw Sister Sophia coming up the street as fast as she could. That she was attempting to run meant that whatever was happening was as alarming as the end of the world, for she was elderly and also suffered from painful knees and shortness of breath. I ran out to meet her, but she continued to move in the direction of her house at the same pace.

'Deannie Dixon,' she panted. 'What you doin' here all by youself, chile?... You don' know dey blastin' de town?'

'Blastin' de town? Who blastin' de town?' I asked with my heart in my mouth.

'Don' ask me, chile;...All I knows is cannonball rollin' in de street, ... smashin' an' burnin' right an' lef'... If not for God in Heaven I be a dead body by now...We got to run away from here quick.'

Before I could question her further, she disappeared into her house. I should have waited for Bro and Daniel, who were certain to return home without delay, but the noise and the smoke and the shouts and screams filled me with such terror that I ran indoors in a state of panic. What was I to take with me? I had prepared a pan of stew the previous evening, but clearly could not take that. Instead, I grabbed a loaf of bread, a jar with steamed oysters, and two ripe mangoes, all of which I wrapped in a kerchief, then looked around for what else might be useful. My agitated mind could make no sensible choices; I rushed outside again and across the street to Sister Sophia's house, calling out to her as I ran. There was no reply and her door stood wide open. Could she have gone without me, I wondered as I entered her front room. To my horror, Sister Sophia was lying slumped against a low cupboard, her legs and skirts all awry. Clouded eyes stared blankly at me. She was plainly beyond my help.

Wailing like a banshee, I fled up the hill, one hand clutching my bundle and the other my right side which had developed a sharp pain all of a sudden. Every breath I took seemed likely to burst my chest wide open, yet I dared not pause even to catch my breath - not until I reached the safety of the forest. Only when I was several feet into the deep green shadows did I stand still, gasping like a fish out of water, my lower legs and ankles scratched and bleeding from the many thorny plants and sharp grasses in the under-growth.

I gradually recovered my breath and my wits and as I did so, realised that I might face greater perils in the forest than from cannonballs. Since that blood-chilling experience of our first days in Freetown, I had never overcome my dread of snakes; it was an unreasonable fear that made me gasp and tremble at the mere sight of one of them slithering around the base of a tree some distance away. Now here I was in their very do-main and heaven alone knew what other dangerous creatures might be lying in wait. With this new fear I wheeled round to return to the town, preferring to meet my fate with the invaders than to face wild animals; the invaders, at least, were humans. I ran and ran, stumbling over roots and over large stones. With my eyes darting here and there, every sense alert to danger, I must have resembled a forest creature myself. Whenever I stopped to catch my breath, I imagined that I could hear explosions amid the many sounds and stirrings of the forest. I would run in the direction of the noise, but never came to the edge of the clearing as I had hoped. I began to whimper as the gloom deepened and I realised that night was falling and I would have to remain in the forest until a new day dawned. However, when it grew dark enough for me no longer to have a choice, a strange calmness descended upon me; perhaps exhaustion mercifully dulled my senses. Whatever the reason, it was without despair that I decided to look for a resting place before total darkness fell.

By some good fortune, I happened upon a large flat rock. Close to trees, but in an area of the forest with sparser vegetation, it was covered in moss and raised above the ground by about two feet. I climbed upon it and sank down, feeling as if I should never again find the strength to descend to the forest floor. Aware that several pairs of eyes must be watching me with suspicion, I slowly opened my kerchief which, for a wonder I had not dropped, broke off a hunk of bread and ate it with the steamed oysters. I then consumed a whole mango, licking my right arm almost to my elbow to catch the last drop of juice. Since there was no way to protect myself against any dangers the night might bring, I curled up on the rock with my knees drawn up to my chin, and wrapped my arms around them. The forest darkened further; the sounds around me increased but, though bone weary, I dared not close my eyes. It was then that the miracle occurred - the first of two that convinced me for all time that God in his greatness still concerned himself with this speck of humanity called Deannie Dixon.

I heard Mammy's voice; heard it as distinctly as if she were sitting next to me on that rock. Three times she said,

'Deannie, girl, de Lord goin' take care of you. Everytin' goin' turn out well, you hear?'

Far from being afraid of her ghost on this occasion, I felt as soothed as if I had just bathed in warm water. I closed my eyes, muttering some of the psalms I knew by heart, just as Mammy herself had done during that terrible storm at sea: 'He that dwelleth in the secret place of the most high shall abide under the shadow of the Almighty. - Thou shalt not fear for the terror by night, nor for the arrow that flieth by day, nor for the pestilence that walketh in darkness, nor for the destruction that wasteth at noon day. The Lord is thy keeper; the Lord is thy shade upon thy right hand. - He that keepeth thee will not slumber. - God is our refuge and strength; a very present help in trouble. Yea, though I walk through the valley of the shadow of death I shall fear no evil. - The God of Jacob is our refuge.'

My face and arms soon burned from bug bites and stings, and from the slaps I gave myself to drive them away, but nothing else happened. I must have fallen asleep eventually, for it seemed that not much time passed before glimmers of light filtered through the leaves, and birds twittered in the trees around me. Morning had come, and I was still alive.

Straightening my limbs from their cramped position was sheer agony. I lay in great discomfort for several minutes before recovering sufficiently to slide down from the rock to ease myself. I climbed up again to eat the rest of my food, thinking I would give my right arm for just one sip of water, and I had begun to wonder, though still with no sense of panic, what would become of me if I could find no way out of the forest. That was when the second miracle occurred.

As I was nearing the end of my breakfast, I heard cautious movements in the tangle of bushes behind me. I turned around slowly, my eyes fixed on the source of the sound. Outwardly, I must have appeared rigid, but my heart was jumping like a small trapped animal, and my gut seemed to be tying itself in knots. Leaves fluttered, a twig cracked under a tread, and then a human hand appeared, followed by a faded blue sleeve. At the same moment that I recognised my brother, Daniel, he let out a joyful cry of, 'Deannie!'

The mango I had been eating fell from my hand. I scrambled down from the rock and, with arms outstretched, ran towards him. It was, however, not Daniel around whom they went, but Junius Porter; on hearing the shout, he had come charging out of the trees, ahead of Daniel.

'Praise be to God,' he murmured as his own arms pressed me against his chest. He soothed me with comforting words while I wept from weakness and relief. Unaware that I was soiling his shirt with the mango juice smeared all over my mouth and hand, I clung to him as if he were saving me from drowning. Eventually my sobs subsided; he raised my chin and smiled into my eyes. I smiled shyly into his, and without any words being spoken, knew for certain that Felicia had told the truth, and that I should seek no further for a husband.

We had all but forgotten Daniel's presence, and hot blood rushed to my cheeks when I became aware of him sitting patiently on my resting place as still as any statue - in the manner, I imagined, it was his custom to be when stalking prey. Freeing myself from Junius's arms, I covered my confusion with
questions.

'Danny, what been happen down dere? Where Bro?'

'Is dem French people,' Daniel said. 'Dey come with day ship done up like English ship.'

'Lord have mercy!' I cried. 'I seen dem! Seven or eight, not so? Dey been come in de harbour... Dem ship belong to French people?'

As Daniel nodded, Junius took up the story.

'When dey done come in de harbor, dey turn cannon on de town an' fire... A terrible tin', Deannie. We was praisin' God when, BOOM! De church wall fall in. Broda Jackson been sittin' down near de wall, he lose he two legs jus' like dat; an' is good he die soon after... You never hear such hollerin' an' cryin' and' prayin'. Everybody tryin' to get out all at once, so nobody able to get out... An' all de time dem big cannonball flyin' everywhere. When we manage to reach outside, Bro say he and Daniel got to go an' fine you; me an' Licia follow dem. When we reach de house we look all roun' but you nowhere. I run across de road to Sista Sophia house; she lyin' dere dead as a stone. So we think maybe you run to de bush or maybe to Pa Demba town. We all go to Pa Demba town...Still no Deannie. Me an' Daniel come back to Freetown, but dem French sailor all over de place, so we hide till night come ; we take Sister Sophia to bury her, den we start lookin' for you again.'

'But how you fine me inside dis big, big bush?' I asked in wonder.

Junius chuckled. 'Is you broda.' He say, "If I knows my coward sista, she been go straight up de hill, not turnin' nowhere till she feel herself safe." So we do just' like dat.

'But after I reach here, I try to go out again. I tink I jus' goin' roun' an' roun' until I lost; so how come you able to fine me so quick?'

'You got to be a hunter like me,' Daniel said, laughing. 'I smell you hair pomade soon as we done come inside de bush. I tell Junius, "Deannie right over dere" - an' here you is, jus' like I say.'

'Danny, is God,' I said with fervour, 'Only God.'

'Is true,' Daniel answered, serious now. 'If not for God, maybe we been lookin' for you till kingdom come ...But why you run off, Deannie, foolish girl? You done make we all worry so.'

'I know, Danny,' I said. 'I so shame; ...I not even stop to make poor Sista Sophia lay down flat... '

I then recounted my own adventures. When I came to the end of my story, Junius said,

'You kin walk, Deannie?'

'Sure I kin walk,' I replied stoutly though, in truth, I was feeling faint from lack of food and water, not to speak of the state of my emotions. 'Where we goin' now?'

'To Pa Demba town.' Junius said. 'We stayin' dere for now... Not too many of we dere; ... maybe some people hidin' in de bush like you, or

dey gone east. Everybody hidin' somewhere because dem Frenchie all over de place;... and dey
wicked!   Goin' roun' breakin' everytin', burnin'
everytin'.... If you see!'

'Why, Why?' I asked. 'What we ever done to
French people?'

'Is not we dey after,' he explained. 'Is dem
Company people because dey fightin' wit Englan',
an' dem Company people English'... But dey too
wicked; behavin' like wile animal.'

'Even wile animal don' behave so,' Daniel
put in disgustedly as we prepared to leave. 'Dey
all crazy wit' liquor.'

'What goin' happen now?' I asked.

'We don' know yet,' Daniel said. 'Pa Demba
town goin' bewe home till dey go ... De ol' man
done give we place to sleep; ...even some Company people stayin' dere. Come on.'

He led the way out of the forest; I followed
with Junius, leaning heavily on his arm, partly
from genuine weakness, but also because the
warmth of his body made me feel safe.

It did not take us long to emerge into bright
sunlight; I could not believe that I had been so
close to the town all along. To avoid the French
sailors, we skirted around the clearing at the foot
of St George's Hill, then passed through another
patch of forest before coming to another clear-

ing. As we stumbled over the rough ground, Junius looked down at me from time to time, saying, 'We goin' reach just' now, you hear?'

Indeed, we soon arrived at a path which they said led to Pa Demba's town. In normal times I would have been looking forward to a new experience, albeit, with some uneasiness, but on this occasion I was too weary to care. All I noticed as we approached the town was a strong smell of smoked fish. Several people, including Bro and Felicia, came rushing up to greet us. Felicia reached me first. I was moved to see the glitter of tears in her eyes as she embraced me.

'Is really my Deannie?' Bro exclaimed as he took me in his arms. 'Praise God Almighty! I been 'fraid we done lost you forever.'

Chapter 19
Interlude

Pa Demba's town. We lived no more than two miles away, yet it could have been another country for all we had known about it before. It was a small place - more a village than a town — with fewer houses than were to be found in Freetown. Their houses were built of mud or clay like ours, but unlike ours, were round instead of square or rectangular. Except for their ragged edges, the roofs bore a resemblance to the fruit of the coconut palm cut in half across the middle.

We had grown accustomed to the inhabitants of Pa Demba's town, and they to us before we had to sojourn there, but it was the first time that we were seeing them at home, so to speak. The men were not much present during the day, but the women and children seemed always to be about, the women being forever occupied either in pounding rice with pestles in narrow wooden mortars, preparing meals in iron cauldrons over wood fires, or else tending their gardens which seemed to grow nothing but dark green leaves and hot peppers. When not engaged in those pursuits, they were going or coming from fetching water; a stream ran close to the town.

We seldom heard young babies cry, which was hardly surprising since they were always either asleep, secured to their mothers' backs with cloths, as observed when we first arrived in Sierra Leone, or else they were contentedly pulling at their mothers' breasts. Most of the older women had slack breasts that hung down almost to their navels - a deformity caused, no doubt, by years of being pulled at by the greedy mouths of their infants. By contrast, the young brides and maidens had beautiful breasts, round and firm through much exercising of their arms.

Their meeting-house, a building larger than the average, served as one of our sleeping quarters. Through its open sides the village children often stood gazing at us with wide-eyed interest. Our loud prayers and boisterous singing seemed to hold a special fascination for them and in a few days they were mimicking our voices and gestures with amusing accuracy. All of daily living was done out of doors in Pa Demba's town, its inhabitants only entering their houses when night fell. I wondered how they lived in the rainy season, but, of course, could not inquire. It was there that I discovered how they wove their hair into the styles that had so fascinated me when we first set foot on these shores.

Each day round about midday, a huge iron cauldron, filled to the brim with steaming boiled rice or cassava, was set before us. A smaller one contained a kind of stew made from their green leaves, smoked fish, and some unknown meat, all swimming in the red oil they extracted from the fruit of a kind of palm tree. It looked unappetizing, but being in no position to turn up our noses at the nourishment on offer, we ate it with gratitude, using our hands as they did, and were pleasantly surprised to find it quite tasty. Not so the Company officials; they rejected the native fare at first, depending solely on mangoes, bananas and coconuts for sustenance till they realised that the French sailors were in no hurry to depart.

A few days after I arrived at Pa Demba's town, Junius, Daniel and Sam Perry decided to return to Freetown, despite tearful pleas from Felicia and myself.

'Don' trouble youself,' Junius said. 'Dey not goin' catch we. We know where to hide...Dey not goin' know where to fine we.'

They set off before dawn, hoping to return before the day was far spent. No sooner was it was light enough than I went and perched on a rock by the path along which I knew they must come, determined to stay there until their return; Felicia joined me later.

I had bitten my fingernails almost to the quick before I observed in the distance three figures making slow and awkward progress towards the village. Each appeared to be carrying a heavy load.

'Licia, you tink' is dem?' I asked hopefully.

'Not sure, Deannie,' she said, but as they drew nearer, agreed that the still distant figures must be Daniel, Junius and Sam Perry. With glad cries, we sped down the path to meet them.

Drenched in sweat and breathing hard, they had triumph written all over their faces. Felicia went to relieve Sam Perry of his load whereas I almost knocked Junius over by flinging myself at him before he had laid his own burden down. He took me in his arms as soon as he could, stopping just short of crushing my ribs.

'Oh, I been so 'fraid for all of you,' I said when I had recovered my breath. 'What you all got dere wrap up like dat?'

'You and Licia, shut you eye one minute,' Daniel said.

So great was my amazement when allowed to open my eyes that for some moments I could only stand and stare, my mouth foolishly agape.

Spread before us were the makings of a feast - a side of salt beef, a side of bacon, molasses, potatoes, onions, cheese, oats; enough to feed us well for some days to come.

'Wh ... where you get all dat from?' Felicia stammered, with equal astonishment.

'Aha. We not sayin' notin," Sam Perry laughed.

'You done stole it from de Company store!' I accused them as realisation dawned.

'Sista, don' give me no talk 'bout no stealin' from no Company,' Sam retorted. 'Who de Company belong to now? We don' even know if Macaulay alive or dead. All de Company buildin' broke or done burn to de groun'. Dem Frenchie killin' even dumb creature - why, I don' know. Already de place stinkin' to high heaven, an,' if you see de fly! Freetown don' belong to no Company no more. It belong to dem Frenchie. Is from dem Frenchie dat we done take de food!'

'But nobody watchin' de store?' Felicia wanted to know.

'Oh, somebody watchin,' Junius answered, 'but dat somebody so beastly drunk on Company rum he sittin' here snorin' like a bull; spit drippin' in he beard. We seen nobody else. Mus' be dey all stupid with liquor, sleepin' somewhere. Come, let we go have weself a feast.'

The young men were welcomed as heroes. Bro declared, 'A right bunch of rascal is what you all be.' But his fond tone and expression belied his words. Everyone, Timmanee and settler alike, gathered round in excited anticipation to see what the heavy bundles contained, and exclamations of delight greeted the appearance of each item. Bro handed a present of rum, molasses and tobacco to old Pa Demba; he grinned with pleasure, showing stumps of teeth stained with tobacco.

At first the Company officials among us looked disapproving of the entire proceedings, but even they could not resist the rich aroma of bacon boiled with onions, potatoes and molasses after subsisting on a diet of fruit and native fare. They partook of the meal we prepared with as much relish as the rest of us and, with their bellies full and their blood warmed by tots of rum. seemed to forget the origin of the provisions.

For the next ten days, our lives followed a similar pattern. Others among the men made sorties into Freetown and brought back whatever they could lay hands on. Pots, pans, buckets, spades, fishing nets, blankets as well as food items, all found their way to Pa Demba's town, and each time, the old man received a present in return for his hospitality. Once we heard that a party of French sailors had been seen near the town; but they never entered it, and I never set eyes on any of them. Not till the middle of October did word reach us that the invaders had at last sailed away and it was safe to return to our homes. It transpired that Governor Macaulay had all the while been a prisoner on one of the French warships. He had been released and, so we heard, persuaded the commander to leave provisions enough to save us from starvation.

I never returned to Pa Demba's town, but my sentiments towards that place and its people remain forever warm. Apart from the hospitality its inhabitants showed us, it was during those days of uncertainty about the future that love for Junius Porter took a hold of me like a tree rooting deeply into the earth. Now that the need for discretion was passed, I could not have enough of gazing at him and soon became so familiar with every detail of his face and person that when I lay down at night and closed my eyes, his image was as clear as if he stood before me.

New love craves solitude but because of our present circumstances, Junius and I were never long alone together in the days following that moment in the forest when we first looked at each other with love. We had to content ourselves with hands clasped under cover of darkness and the exchange of telling glances till the day Felicia and I announced our intention to fetch water from the stream in his presence. Junius offered to help us carry the buckets and I guessed that he was creating an opportunity to have me to himself. Indeed, who had ever heard of a man offering to carry water when there were young women present and well able to perform that task? My heart seemed to turn right over.

Knowing how matters stood between us, like me, Felicia must have guessed his intention; but she neither made a comment nor gave us a knowing look. However, once we reached the stream, she said,

'I goin' full dem bucket real slow, an' two of you kin go see where dis water comin' from.'

Junius smacked a kiss on her cheek, saying,

'Licia, you de best sista in dis whole worl'!'

She gave him a little push of dismissal and he took my hand. As we strolled happily away, she called out, 'Deannie Dixon, 'member what you been promise you Mammy...'

Had my complexion been lighter, it surely would have turned as crimson as a cherry, for I expected Junius in the next instant to ask me what Felicia meant by that remark; he merely chuckled. Once out of sight of Felicia, he tightened his grip on my hand and said with unusual gravity,

'Deannie, up yonder, inside de bush, you not jus' feelin' happy because me and Daniel done fine you?'

'No, Junius, no; not dat alone,' I answered as earnestly as he had asked the question. 'All dat time when you been comin' by de house, I been tink 'bout you always like you is my broda ... I never tink 'bout love or anytin' between me an' you till Licia tell me sometin'; ... An' I not been believe what she done tell me.'

'You believe now?' Junius wanted to know. I nodded, adding, though I found it most difficult to speak of such things, 'When you come in de bush to fine me, an' by how you been hol' me; ... is from dat time I done believe. I knows I don' want to marry to nobody but you.'

'You sure, Deannie? You not goin' say sometin' else when we done go back home? ... I know I not up to much; ... not able to read good like you an' Daniel.'

I silenced him with my fingers on his lips, and the leaping light in his eyes filled me with joy.

'I know me mine, Junius, an' I never goin' change. I goin' be happy to be you wife if you want to marry to me.'

'If?... Listen dis woman!' he cried out to the trees and the sky, at the same time pressing my shoulders so hard that I winced. 'Deannie Dixon, Licia not been tell you dat I done want you from de firs' day I seen you? ... All de time I comin' to you house is because I dyin' for you ... Licia been say you jus' a small girl an' I got to wait a while.'

'But, Junius, all de time you been jestin' wit' me, even when I done big more ... How you been tink I goin' know how you feelin'? ...Nobody kin see inside no oda person head .'

'Is true,' he agreed. 'If you been know how I torment, Deannie ... When you done big more, you done so use to me like you broda, I don' know how to make you look me differen' ... An' again, I been tellin' myself if Bro fine out, he goin' tell me not to come to de house no more because he don' want no lab'rer for he son-in-law. Deannie, what I been pass through, even hell not goin' be so bad.'

By this time, I was smiling to think how similar to my own thoughts had been the reasons for his maddening reticence.

"What you smilin' for?' he asked, his voice now low and strange, his light eyes of a sudden intensely bright. 'Hmm? What you smilin' for?'

Without waiting for an answer, he drew me fully into his arms and began to kiss me.

Ah, the power of passion! Not a thought did I give to my loathsome enemies of old; for all I cared in the moments that followed, one of them could have slithered up to us and wished us good day. At the touch of Junius Porter's lips upon mine, strange new sensations swept over me with such force that I clung to him as tightly as I had done in the forest. In response, he pressed the whole length of his body against mine and continued to kiss me till we were both breathless and trembling and scarcely able to stand. Not a thought did I give to my promise to Mammy; for all knew at the time, I might already have broken it and must confess, with regret, that I did not care. It was Junius who first loosened his grip on me, and when I still would have clung to him, held me at arms' length, whispering, 'No, Deannie, no;... 'member what you been promise you Mammy.'

It seemed that I had not broken my promise after all - that what had just happened between us was not the 'carrying on' Mammy had feared, though there was clearly a connection.

'How you know what I been promise Mammy?' I asked.

'I jus' knows,' Junius answered in his normal voice. 'Jus' by how Licia been say, "Deannie Dixon, don' you forget what you been promise you Mammy!"'

His perfect imitation of Licia's voice made me fall into his arms again, weak with love and laughter. He joined in my laughter, but quickly pushed me away.

'Deannie, listen.' he said. 'You Mammy been a woman wit' plenty good sense ... She been know you a sweet innocent. Man kin make you give youself befo' you knows what happenin' to you. I want for you to feel proud of youself till you die, not feelin' shame inside. I knows you goin' feel shame inside if you don' follow what you promise you Mammy.' He paused for a moment to give me a stern look - the same kind Bro used to give me when I had committed some childish misdemeanour. 'We got to do sometin' 'bout you an' me so you not goin' regret 'til you die ... You know what, I not goin' kiss you an' hol' you like jus' now no more.'

'No more?' I cried; I felt extremely disappointed.

'No more,' he said with a firm shake of his head. 'Not 'til we done wed good an' proper... Goin' be hard, but I want you too much and maybe nex' time I not goin' be able to stop... You know what we goin' do? When I come callin' we goin' sit out on de porch. Yes; an' when we go for a stroll, we goin' stroll down Broad Street, front of everybody.'

I was ignorant of all that to which Junius was referring, but took his careful plans to be a measure of the regard in which he held me. My adoration must have shone through my eyes, for all of a sudden he said as fiercely as Pastor George on the pulpit,

'Deannie Dixon, I trying to help you, but you not helpin' me one bit ... I swear, if you look me like dat again, you goin' make me forget everytin' I done say jus' now.'

My response was to throw myself into his arms again, saying, 'Junius Porter, you de mos' wonderful man in dis whole worl'!'

'Dat's de truth,' he said, his old jesting self again. 'An' we better go on back befo' ol' Satan start workin' to change me ...An' Deannie, promise me we goin' be wed soon - jus' as soon as we done settle down again.'

I gave him my word, and he rewarded me with a kiss on my forehead as gentle as the touch of a feather.

Hands on hips, Felicia looked from one to the other when we finally rejoined her.

'Two of you been gone a long time,' she said in a tone of mock severity. 'Deannie, I goin' tell Broda Dixon he better get you wed just now if he want for poor Mammy to rest easy where she lyin.'

We laughed together, well content.

We asked for Bro's consent after evening prayers. If he was disappointed in my choice, he did not betray it by so much as a slight change of his countenance. On the contrary, having given us his blessing, he put an arm around Junius's shoulders and said, 'So dat why you been comin' to my house, an' all de time I tink you comin' to visit wit me an' Daniel. You a sly one, Junius Porter.'

To me, he said, ' Deannie, jus' you try an' be like you Mammy, you hear? If you be like her, Junius Porter goin' be de mos' happiest man in Freetown.'

Chapter 20
Starting afresh

The Freetown we returned to was a most unpleasant place. Even before we arrived, the stench of rotten flesh assailed our nostrils. In the hot weather this miasma hung about the place for days, even after all the swollen and maggot-ridden carcasses of the animals had been buried. Fat green flies rested on every surface; vultures sat on the roofs and branches, having gorged their fill. I could not understand how so-called civilised people could have conducted themselves in so despicable and savage a manner, even if they were at war with England.

Apart from the devastation Daniel, Junius and others had already described, we discovered, as we walked around the town, that even the churches had not been spared. All the pulpits were shattered, hymnals ripped apart, and in the Company church, the huge leather-bound Bible from which the lessons were read had been slashed in several places. Our small library had been burned to the ground with only a few charred remains of the volumes therein left to show that it had ever existed.

It was with sickened hearts that we began the attempt to restore order out of that chaos - an impossible task, it seemed. Fortunately, except in a few instances, most of our own houses had been spared the ravages of fire though they had been thoroughly ransacked and plundered.

Not a single one of my chickens was left alive, and as for my gardens, they were a tangle of trampled plants, withered leaves and dead flowers. I could have wept, yet had to be thankful that the house itself was still standing.

Tempers flared easily in the weeks following our return and quarrels with the Governor started all over again, what with the rumours that had circulated during our brief exile in Pa Demba's town. One had it that Governor Macaulay had offered our properties to the French sailors in exchange for sparing the Company's property, another that he had pleaded with the French Commander to take us all away, and yet another that theCompany stores had contained large quantities of goods which well-wishers in England had sent out for us, but which the Governor had been keeping from us.

'Dat Gov'nor, he bad!' Bro said, 'but I doubt even he goin' do all dem tin' dey sayin'.'

Most people agreed with him, but there were some only too glad of yet another opportunity to challenge Governor Macaulay. That gentleman did not help matters either. In his usual manner, he issued a decree that all Company property stolen during the French occupation should be returned forthwith, that those who failed to comply would be deprived of their employment as well as all Company services, including medical attention and schooling for their children. The matter was hotly debated for days on end. Even people not actively against Company rule believed that this time the Governor had gone too far.

'Don' know what dat Macaulay man talkin' 'bout,' Bro said, echoing Sam Perry's words in Pa Demba's Town. 'He done surrender to dem French people. If dem Frenchie been catch dem as been takin' provision an' Company property what Macaulay been able to do to save dem? Notin!'

The Governor had asked that everyone willing to restore the Company's property put his signature or mark to the decree. No more than one hundred people signed, and when he carried out his threat to dismiss those who refused to sign, he discovered that the people of Freetown had changed since the early part of the year. Having realised that, at best, the Company could afford them only limited protection, they sought to become more independent of Company rule. A man called Gideon John, among others, opened a private school; those children whose disobedient parents disqualified them from attending the Company's school attended classes there instead. Some people even dared to leave Freetown altogether; they acquired farm land from the Timmanees. Pastor Luke Jordan moved out to a place called Pirates' Bay, some miles further west. Others, who could no longer work for the Company and had already, received their farm land, turned properly to farming near the old Granville Town and on the slopes of St. George's Hill.

However, due to changed circumstances, relations between the Company and the citizens of Freetown began to improve after a while. Governor Dawes's return from his leave and Zachary Macaulay's departure on his played a part, as well as the continuing war against the French. Many Company officials were ordered back to England, forcing the Governor to use more of our people in responsible positions. He appointed a man called, James Edmonds, under-surgeon, another called, Jesse George, assistant apothecary; and, for the first time, he allowed settlers to purchase goods wholesale so they could start a retail trade with the Timmanees. Some of our people found trading so much to their liking, that they abandoned all thoughts of becoming farmers.

Since French vessels were sighted along the coast from time to time, people now readily volunteered their labour when the Governor decreed that, in view of the invasion of the previous year, Freetown's defences should again be strengthened. As a further demonstration of his growing confidence in the citizens of Freetown, he decided to form a militia composed of all able-bodied men. Junius, Daniel, and even Bro, had to attend firing practice twice a week, and Daniel, on account of his expertise with a gun was made a lieutenant. In the Freetown of January, 1794, the Governor would never have armed settlers for fear that they would turn their guns on Company officials. It was in that cordial atmosphere that a better Freetown began to rise from the ruins of the old.

A large court house was being built on Broad Street, at the same time as a new church, large enough to seat a thousand people. Two hospitals had been built, as well as new houses for Company officials and another subscription library. Some of our own people either improved their old houses or built new ones with stone foundations and shingled roofs. With all the new construction, it was a time of modest prosperity for Bro, that expert carpenter. He invited Junius to join himself and Daniel in the enterprise, initially as an apprentice, but with a view to partnership when he became fully competent. He also built his own carpentry workshop adjoining our house and, in front of the building put up a large sign with the words DIXON AND SONS boldly painted in red. Beneath, in smaller letters it read:

'Carpenters for the Living and the Dead.Use our services for strong houses, and fine furniture.Sympathetic and Respectful undertaking Coffins delivered in four hours.'

In the six months before we were wed, Junius became a busy man, for in addition to his apprenticeship with my father, he was engaged, with Daniel's help, in extending his own house on Wilberforce Street so that we might have a larger bedchamber. One evening, we strolled along Broad Street as far as the Governor's residence and, arm in arm, enjoyed the sunset which had turned the quiet waters of St George's Bay to polished bronze.

'Deannie,' he said, 'two year from today, know what goin' happen?'

'No, what?'

'I goin' start on a house wit' a stone cellar, an a roof wit' shingle; an' you goin' have a servant to clean an' cook an' go to de store.'

'What I goin' be doin' den?' I asked, amused. 'I not use to idle life.'

'You goin' be busy bornin' children, one after de oda till you have ten; but you kin carry on wit' you dressmakin'... When evenin' come, you goin' keep school jus' for me, an' help me to read an' write till I kin do it better dan you.'

'An' what *you* goin' be doin', Junius Porter?'

'Me?' he said carelessly, 'I goin' be workin' hard to make you de mos' happiest wedded woman in Freetown.'

Out in the open, in full view of the world, I could only attempt to show him my heart with my eyes.

CHAPTER 21
My nuptials and beyond

The firing of the cannon woke me as usual at half- past the hour of five in the morning. It was the fifteenth day of May, 1795, my seventeenth birthday and also my wedding day. However, no one seeing me on that morning would have thought that I was about to become the happiest woman in Freetown. Instead of joy, I had awoken with my spirits so thoroughly weighed down by feelings of anxiety and sadness that I could hardly bestir myself to go outside and start the fire. In one so lacking in bravery as I, the anxiety was easy to understand; I was going to become a wife that day, and having at last summoned the courage to confess my ignorance to Felicia had learnt in what manner 'carrying on' took place. My utter dejection was less easy to explain.

I read from the Bible that morning when the three of us, Bro, Daniel and I, came together to have prayers as a family for the last time; afterwards, we knelt down and Bro prayed with special fervour for his little girl who was about to be wed without her mother to advise her. As his voice faltered over the words, my eyes filled with tears. My sadness centred on Mammy's absence, and I began to weep in earnest. Bro's arm encircled my shaking shoulders and held me to him as he completed his prayer.

'Deannie, I know how you feelin' today,' he said when we rose. 'My own heart heavy like yours, but is de Lord's will for Mammy to be gone away. Is de Lord's will.'

I simply nodded, still unable to speak. Bro gave my shoulders another squeeze. 'Jus' you make sure she goin' be proud of her girl wherever she be, you hear?'

Daniel, meanwhile, had gone out to the porch and was leaning on the ledge, staring at the ocean; what his thoughts and emotions were I could only imagine. He came back inside after a few minutes, but only to tell us that he was going out to the shop to work for a while on a sofa he was making. Bro drank a dish of tea and went out to join him; sadly, I went about my household tasks for the last time. In future, Daniel and Bro would have to fend for themselves except for their main meal which I would continue to prepare for them.

Felicia arrived in the middle of the morning, already dressed for the wedding in a dress of turquoise muslin, with lace at the wrist and neck, and a bonnet to match. The costume showed to perfection the velvety texture of her golden skin.

'How de little bride?' she called out as she came swaying through the door. I did not respond and, taking a closer look at me, she said,

'Grievin' for her Mammy... Deannie, listen, I knows how you feelin' today, but notin' goin' to bring Mammy back. Sure you feelin' low, but Junius out dere waitin' for you, prettyin' heself up for you, an' you want to go meet him wit' you face like de middle of July? Well, I not goin' let you. Where you keep rum in dis house?'

'Licia, I don' want no liquor,' I said in a tone as listless as I felt.

'You goin' drink it,' she said. 'Soon I goin' be you sista— you big sista; you got to do what I tells you. Where de rum... hmm?'

I pointed out the cupboard and she went herself to fetch the bottle. Having poured about a tot into a cup, she said,

'Drink it all de way down; one swallow...It goin' make you eye shine again.'

It was with a reproachful look that took the cup from her, but I did as told. It was the first time hard liquor had passed my lips. I found the taste abominable and for a few moments thought my head would burst asunder as the fiery liquid seared its way down my throat. I coughed, I spluttered, but as it coursed through my body, just as Felicia had promised, my spirits began to rise. Felicia had poured herself a tot and, within minutes, we were laughing merrily together. I said,

'Better put dat rum back befo' Bro come in or he goin' say you spoilin' he lil girl and refuse for me to join de Porter fam'ly.'

'Pooh!' Licia said, not in the least repentant. 'I goin' turn he lil girl into a proper woman. Notin' to beat a tot when you spirit droopin'. Now go wash youself so we kin start makin' you look good for Junius.'

I had spent months preparing my trousseau and now owned calico bed sheets, pillow cases embroidered with flowers and Bible texts, half a dozen shifts and knickers, three new dresses and my wedding dress which, though not of a rich fabric, looked well on me. Low-necked and full-skirted, it was made of white sprigged muslin, specially ordered by my intended. Felicia had trimmed my bonnet with French lace and my white satin slippers, a gift from Bro, displayed large gilt buckles at the toes.

Felicia helped me dress, then having kissed my cheek stood back to admire her handwork.

'I swear to God, my broda not goin' listen to one word Pastor George sayin',..He goin' be too busy lookin' at you, an' lookin' forward to the night.'

'Licia Porter, you no good,' I said, but promptly belied that remark by thanking her for bringing Junius and me together.

'You not happy more dan me, Deannie,' she said. 'I jus' selfish; I want two people I love to be under de same roof as me...You 'fraid, girl?'

'Lil bit,' I confessed.

'No need to be,' she said. 'Junius a good, kind person, even if I says it. He not goin' be rough wit' you; ... Don' trouble you mine, you hear?'

I emerged from my bedchamber to find Bro sitting in the front room with a neighbour from down the street. Daniel, who was standing as Junius's best man, had long since departed for the church. Bro rose to his feet at once, gazing at me with immense tenderness and pride, while the neighbour performed a comical charade of being so dazzled by the sight of me that he could hardly bear to look in my direction. His antics prevented what could have been another sad moment. We were still chuckling when Bro held up his arm. I hooked mine through it and we stepped out of the door. To my amazement, a cheer went up as soon as we appeared on the porch, for a small crowd had gathered in the street, quite prepared to accompany me to church.

Though hot and humid as ever, it was a fitting day for a bride. Clouds like oversized cotton balls hung low in the sky, their whiteness intensifying the clear blue beyond. Felicia opened an umbrella over me, and we three proceeded slowly to avoid undue bursts of perspiration. Down Howe Street we sauntered, and along Cross Street to its corner with Wilberforce Street, where our little church stood. By the time we arrived at the door I was perfectly composed. Not even the sight of the guests, who filled the

church to bursting, ruffled my calmness.We proceeded up the aisle, Bro and I, with Felicia following. Up ahead stood Pastor George, beaming
from the altar table, but I gave him scarcely a
glance. My gaze settled on the straight-backed
figure standing beside Daniel by the first row of
pews — Junius, with whom all my future lay; Junius who, as we reached his side, turned slightly
towards me, smiled into my eyes and whispered,
'You ready?' I nodded with a smile. He took my
gloved fingers tightly in his warm hand and we
walked to the altar.

Chapter 22
The following years

So, dear reader, I married Junius Porter, and never have I felt a moment of regret. My husband proved to be the most demanding and persevering of pupils. Within a year his ability to read surpassed my own, and I am proud to say that he is now an inspiring lay preacher. Under Bro's expert tutelage, he also became an excellent carpenter, and when Bro went to join my beloved Mammy in 1810, he and Daniel became partners in the family business. They abandoned the undertaking side of it to concentrate on erecting furnished dwellings which they let out to the ever increasing number of Company officials.

Junius kept his promise to me though it took much more than two years to fulfil; I am now the mistress of a house with a stone cellar, a proper floor, and a shingled roof. However, we have not been without our share of sorrow. I did bear ten children but, before they left the cradle, our five little sons perished from one of the many sicknesses that plague this place; only our five daughters have survived. Yet I cannot complain. The good Lord has blessed and protected us over the years in ways too numerous to mention here.

Daniel has never married, but Felicia and Sam Perry were wed in 1802. By that time Felicia was the mother of two high-spirited boys; but it was only when Sam promised that she would not have to concern herself with his fishing business that she agreed to surrender her freedom. They, too, have prospered. As the years went by, Sam acquired three fishing boats and employed younger men to go out to sea on his behalf. Nowadays, he goes down to the seashore only to supervise the sale of his catch. A few years past, he and Felicia obtained a licence to operate an ale-house. Thanks to the merry nature of its owners, it has become one of the best patronised in Freetown.

And what of Freetown itself? The more harmonious relations we enjoyed with the Company after the French invasion did not last, mainly because, once again, ill-health forced Governor Dawes to return to England and the overbearing Zachary Macaulay returned. During this tour of duty, the main cause of his conflict with our people was the matter of quit-rents. While we were yet in Nova Scotia, Governor Clarkson had promised that grants of land would be given free of charge. It later transpired that he had no authority to make such a promise on behalf of the Sierra Leone Company. Nevertheless, he had made the promise; so, when the Company first demanded a rent of one shilling an acre, nobody agreed to pay it. Zachary Macaulay decided that the time had come to enforce payment and straightaway, came into sharp conflict with the die-hard opponents of Company rule. Up until 1799 when he left Freetown never to return, he had not succeeded in collecting any quit-rents, despite the many penalties he devised for failure to pay.

During his second term as Governor, the Hundredors and Tythingmen asked to be allowed, from time to time, to suggest new laws for the governing of Freetown. Unexpectedly, Zachary Macaulay agreed to the request and even adopted some of the laws they suggested. Having tasted some power, the more rebellious among them agitated for more, saying that the Company should concern itself with matters of trade only and leave the government of Freetown entirely in the hands of the Hundredors and Tythingmen. Thomas Ludlum - a less determined individual, had replaced Zachary Macaulay as governor by that time. Under him, the agitation for greater power grew to an open rebellion led by four Hundredors: Isaac Anderson, who was one of the two elected to take that ill-fated petition to the Company Directors in 1793, James Robertson, Nathaniel Wansey and Anzel Zizer.

If I remember rightly, it was in September, 1800, that they went so far as to make a formal declaration of independence. It stated' that Freetown belonged to its Negro citizens, that henceforth, all Europeans would be considered foreigners and as such, would be required to obey the laws drawn up by the Hundredors and Tythingmen. Governor Ludlum sent to have the four ringleaders arrested, but after an exchange of gunfire only James Robertson and Anzel Zizer were captured. Isaac Anderson and Nathaniel Wansey escaped and formed a rebel army which assembled at the east end of Freetown. With a handful of supporters, Governor Ludlum formed an army of his own. It pitched camp on Thornton Hill (once called St. George's Hill).

As usual, the rest of the citizenry, desiring peace much more than they desired independence, waited safely indoors to see which of the two armies would prevail. At first it appeared that Company rule might be about to end in Freetown but then, as if by heavenly intervention, a ship arrived. When its passengers disembarked, we discovered that it had brought, not only a party of British soldiers with their bright red coats almost glowing in the sunlight, but also a large number of the fiercest looking Negroes I had ever laid eyes on. Unkempt hair added to their fearsome appearance, and all the men fairly bristled with arms: muskets, knives and cutlasses. We later learned that they, too, were former slaves and had come from a faraway place in the West Indies called Jamaica; they were known as Maroons and had stubbornly refused to remain enslaved. To get rid of their troublesome presence the British sent them to Nova Scotia but, like us, they had found Canada much too cold and demanded relocation.

Their arrival saved the Governor. Joining forces with the British soldiers, they vanquished the rebels with little difficulty. Isaac Anderson was eventually hanged and, as a result of the rebellion, the offices of Hundredor and Tythingman were abolished. Thus one step forward had ended in several steps backward. Instead of the independence some craved, the citizens of Freetown had no further say in its government.

As if the trouble between the rebels and the Company were not enough, our Timmanee neighbours now demanded the return of the land on which Freetown was built. At the time, we thought their demand unreasonable, but I have since learned that, according to their own understanding of such matters, it was entirely justified. The directors of the Sierra Leone Company thought they had purchased the land upon which they founded our colony, whereas according to their custom, the Timmanee king had merely granted them permission to use it, expecting to receive the courtesy due a landlord. He and his subjects therefore bitterly resented not being consulted about plans for fortifications and such, as well as the fact that, though the Company had opened a school for their children, the presence of Timmanees in Freetown was barely tolerated. They considered it the final insult when more British soldiers landed on these shores and, without so much as a by-your-leave, began to build a fort on Thornton Hill.

By this time, King Tom had succeeded King Jimmy in the country to the west. Towards the end of 1801, he marched on Freetown with his warriors, and it took a long, fierce battle to drive them back. The reader may easily imagine our fear and trembling as, barricaded into our fragile houses, we prayed for God's mercy. In revenge, the British soldiers and Maroons invaded King Tom's country, forcing the inhabitants to flee from their villages. The next year, King Tom tried to take his own revenge, but once again his warriors were no match for the forces aiding the Governor.

Such tit for tat battles continued for nearly seven years, and we lived in fear that King Bai Farama, who now ruled in the north, would join forces with King Tom. Governor Ludlum had high stone walls built all along our land boundaries and, apart from the fearless Maroons, only a few brave souls dared to venture outside them. Many people abandoned their farms and, once again, food became scarce. Imagine our relief, dear reader, when the Timmanees realised they would never prevail against the superior arms of the Company's forces, and accepted a peace treaty. They agreed to give up all the land captured from them to the west of Freetown, as well as several small villages along the waterfront to the east.

By that time, having suffered one hindrance after another to realising profits from their enterprise, the directors of the Sierra Leone Company must have decided to give up the struggle. I have no idea what happened behind the scenes, but on New Year's Day, 1808, it was the Union Jack and not the Company's flag that we saw flying over the Governor's residence on Thornton Hill.

The year before that, the British Government had finally outlawed the trade in African slaves. Since then, British warships have been patrolling our waters. They attack outlaw British slavers as well as those of other nationalities, and rescue the poor souls who have been captured from up and down the coast, some, I have no doubt, from villages not far from here. These recaptives are released in Freetown and, for obvious reasons, are called Liberated Africans.

I am glad that they are being saved from a life of slavery but wish they could have been taken elsewhere. For one thing, though I have heard tell that a good few are God-fearing Mohammedans, most of them seem to be pagans, some with ugly scars disfiguring their cheeks. For another thing, not one word of a civilised tongue do any of them speak. At the rate they keep arriving on these shores, they will soon outnumber us, and I am afraid our community will change for the worse in just the way Governor Macaulay once warned when talking about the harmful influence of the Timmanees.

My husband scolds me whenever I voice those fears, telling me to remember that we, Nova Scotians, have no reason to feel superior to anyone, considering that our own parents were once unlettered slaves. He reminds me of the progress the Maroons have made due to our influence (apart from their fierceness, they used to be addicted to bloody cock-fighting contests and had several wives at the same time. Now, many of them are Christians; they have even built themselves a fine church). Mr. Porter says that if Maroons could be converted so can the newcomers and that instead of keeping them at arms' length, we should accept their presence in our midst as there is plenty of room for us all. He keeps urging me to start a school for the older ones, now that our girls are grown.

'Is de only way, Deannie,' he insists. 'Somebody been learn you; now you got to learn somebody else; an' I know you kin do it. After all you done practise wit' me... We got to raise dem up so Freetown kin be a good place for all of we, not sit down an' grumble an' wish dey been take dem some place else. If we raise dem up, dis place goin' be famous down de coas' an' in Englan' even.'

In spite of my misgivings, I have to agree that his attitude is the only sensible one and, no doubt, I shall submit to his persuasion before long. When Mr. Porter is convinced of the rightness of a course of action I have always been like potter's clay in his hands. That timid young man of twenty-five years ago has long ceased to exist.

The End

Acknowledgements

I wish gratefully to acknowledge the guidance I received from the following books and papers:

Falconbridge, A. M. Two voyages to Sierra Leone. London, 1794.

Fyfe, C. A history of Sierra Leone. Oxford U.P. 1962.

Fyfe, C.Thomas Peters: history and legend.

Sierra Leone Studies (N.S.) 1 1953.

Haliburton, G. The Nova Scotian settlers of 1792. Sierra Leone Studies (N.S.) 9 1957.

Kirk-Greene, A. David George and the Nova Scotian experience. Sierra Leone Studies(N.S.) 14 1960.

Kup, A. P. Freetown in 1794. Sierra Leone Studies (N.S.) 11 1958.

Peterson, J. Province of Freedom. Faber, 1969. Walker, J. W. St. G. The Black Loyalists. Longman/Dalhousie U.P. 1976.

Y.L.H.